Don't Tell Him I'm a Mermaid

Also by Laura Kirkpatrick

And Then I Turned into a Mermaid

For Al and Brodie,

even though you both

consider mermaids to be deeply uncool.

CHAPTER
1

The Faulty... Thingamajig

Molly Seabrook's favorite thing about being a mermaid was sharing the unlikely secret with her sisters. She had four of them in all, and even though Molly found at least seventy-five percent of them deeply irritating, it was quite nice to have a special family bond. Plus, if any of them stole her white chocolate, she could slap them in the face with her tail, which was definitely a perk.

The worst thing about being a mermaid was almost everything else.

Kittiwake Keep, the wonky old lighthouse they called home, was in pandemonium.

Mom had, for reasons unknown, finally decided to attempt to fix the broken dishwasher. The broken dishwasher had been broken for years, but it didn't particularly matter, because its primary purpose was not to wash dishes. It was to disguise the trapdoor hidden beneath it that led straight into the sea.

In any case, Mom had obviously gotten tired of the endless stacks of mugs beside the sink, so she rolled up her sleeves, donned her rubber gloves, and took a wrench to the faulty...thingamajig.

It did not work.

The dishwasher was now essentially a furious geyser, spraying water all over the kitchen. The swordfish wallpaper was drenched, the sink was overflowing, and Molly felt like she was trapped inside a washing machine.

Myla, her eldest sister and a literal genius, was frantically leafing through the owner's manual—which was now dripping wet and bleeding ink—as though it contained the key to her Cambridge entrance exam. Margot, the second-oldest at sixteen and a notorious practical joker, found the entire thing hilarious and was currently livestreaming it via YouTube. Melissa, Molly's painfully earnest fourteen-year-old roommate, was lecturing Mom on the importance of hiring professionals.

Minnie, who was six, sat at the soaking kitchen table and laughed like a hyena for around twenty minutes.

Unfortunately, the room was becoming so wet that the

inevitable was surely about to happen. They were about to transform into mermaids, as they did whenever they got too close to a body of water. Or puddles. Or broken toilets.

They were about to transform, and Minnie did not know their secret.

"Minnie, can you please go and fetch the house phone?" Mom asked in a strangled voice as she accidentally swallowed another mouthful of dirty dishwater.

"Are you calling the water police?" Minnie cackled.

"Yes," Melissa sighed. "Exactly. The water police."

"They have special handcuffs," Margot added seriously.

"Can you go now, please?" Mom asked through gritted teeth.

As she felt her legs begin to tingle, Molly gripped the edge of the kitchen counter. Minnie splashed happily out into the corridor mere seconds before Molly's stark white tail sprang into place.

"Barricade," Mom barked. "Now."

Right as she was about to transform, Margot charged at a dining chair like a football player, shoving it along the floor until it slammed into the door. Unfortunately, her tail materialized right at the last minute, and she face planted the wet floor with a *splosh* and an *ooft*.

"Do. Not. Let. Her. In." Melissa panted with the effort of

holding herself upright on her buttercup-yellow tail. "Under any circumstances!"

This may have seemed like an extreme reaction, but it was absolutely paramount that Minnie did not uncover the truth too soon. The mermaids had an agreement with the human government that they were allowed to live on land as long as they kept their true identities hidden. If the secret got out, they'd be banished back to Meire, the old mermaid queendom. Meire was now too dirty and dangerous to live in, thanks to pollution and...poop. A lot of human poop.

There was no way Minnie would be able to hold her tongue if she found out her mom and sisters were mermaids and that she, too, would become one on her thirteenth birthday. For instance, after Mom gave her the talk about how she had a different dad, she went around telling the entire town that her dad was the "predisent" of the United States but that her sisters were peasants. So, there was no way something of this magnitude would stay secret.

"Heyyyy!" Minnie yelled, pounding on the closed door with her tiny—and probably sticky—fist. "Let me in! Not fair!"

"We're having a grown-up chat, Minnie," Melissa called. "We'll be out in a moment."

The door began to budge with the weight of a six-year-old

flinging her full force against it, but Margot launched herself up with her poppy-red tail and plonked down into the barricade chair just in time. Minnie wailed in frustration.

Just then, the doorbell rang. Mom exchanged worried glances with Myla.

"The delivery," Myla groaned, wriggling her emerald-green tail. Her wet hair was plastered to her forehead, and her glasses were covered in spray. "I ordered all those secondhand textbooks to be delivered today."

"They'll go away in a minute. Don't worry," Mom said, dutifully ignoring the fact that she was being squirted in the face by a spiteful appliance. "They'll just leave one of those slips saying it's with a neighbor or something."

"Or Minnie will go and let them in," Myla whispered in horror.

"Quick! Knock her out with your tail!" Margot said to Molly, knowing how much her sister enjoyed using her tail as a weapon.

"Okay, can we all just—"

Mom's words were cut off by a fresh spray of water to the face and a nervous tap on the kitchen window.

It was the deliveryman, peering right into a room full of mermaids.

Ever the quick thinker, Margot dove toward the

dishwasher and whirled it around to face the window so the gushing cascade of water sprayed straight into the glass and obscured the deliveryman's vision. Such a feat would normally be impossible, but Margot's merpower—for each mermaid has a special gift—was superhuman strength. Myla's was being able to read sea languages without ever having to study, while Melissa's was being a know-it-all, i.e., being able to tell whenever someone was lying.

"I'll come back later then," the deliveryman called meekly through the glass.

"Do you think he saw?" Melissa gasped. "Oh no, oh no, oh no. What if he saw, Mom?"

"Was it the deliveryman? I didn't see," Mom said, but she was chewing her bottom lip, and Molly could tell she was genuinely worried about being banished.

Molly's stomach twisted. She hadn't exactly done a fantastic job of keeping the whole tail thing under wraps.

She'd only found out about her life as a half mermaid on her thirteenth birthday, a mere two months ago, and yet she'd already accidentally transformed in front of Felicity Davison, the most popular girl in school. There was a whole mess that involved taking a penguin hostage, but Felicity had eventually agreed not to tell anyone Molly's secret—as long as Molly promised not to spread the word about Felicity's mom's cancer. Molly only knew about Mrs. Davison's illness thanks to her own merpower: reading people's emotions. She would never have told anyone something so personal, especially having been through it with her own mom, but Felicity didn't trust her. Their truce was a shaky one, and Molly lived in fear of Felicity going back on her word.

"Can I come in yet?" Minnie asked. "I need to poop."

CHAPTER

2

Like, Superhot in a Totally Athletic Way

The next morning at school, Molly was convinced she smelled of ancient dishwasher fluid. All through math class, she kept quietly sniffing herself as if trying to figure out whether she'd remembered to use deodorant. Her best friend, Ada, stared at her as though she might have contracted leprosy in the night. Ada was very glamorous and cool and had probably never smelled like an old dishwasher in her life.

Ms. Stavros was really trying her very hardest to make pre-algebra interesting. The Sterling School for Promising Little Marmouthians (SPLuM to its students) was one of those "outstanding" places where the teachers all care very deeply, which Molly found pretty irritating, because it meant you were supposed to care too.

It wasn't that she hated school for no reason. It was just

that everything they learned was boring, and she could never hold her concentration for more than five seconds, and it seemed like everyone had a special interest except her.

Lately, whenever her attention drifted in class, she invariably began to think about mermaid life. While she'd initially been absolutely mortified by the entire thing—and to be honest, having a fish tail was still *vaguely gross*—now curiosity itched at her like a woolly sweater. Her mind kept meandering down to Meire, wondering what the magical queendom had been like in its heyday, before the pollution and the poop. Mermaids used to live there by choice, after all, and if clamdunk—the energetic national sport—was anything to go by, it was all very magical and strange.

As humiliating as the spontaneous transformations were, Molly found herself wanting to know more about this other side of her life. She wanted to experiment with her merpower, try out clamdunk for herself, and maybe even make a few mermaid friends beyond her family. And yet Molly was also incredibly stubborn. She had always insisted to her mom and sisters that their secret was deeply, deeply embarrassing, and she didn't want to have to admit that she was secretly a little curious.

At lunch, Molly plonked herself down at her usual table beside Margot. The cafeteria workers had decided to branch out with today's menu, and Molly prodded what she'd been assured was a vol-au-vent with her fork. It was the least appetizing hunk of dry pastry Molly had ever seen. She supposed you could use it to plug a hole in a broken dishwasher.

"Hello, dearest sister," Margot said, crunching through her own vol-au-vent in such a violent manner that it sprayed all over her face. "How doth you be today?"

"What?"

Margot rolled her eyes. "We've been doing Shakespeare. It has been physically painful. Why can't he just speak English?"

"Mmm," Molly mumbled.

"What's wrong?" Margot asked. She was assembling a prank involving a catapult and a fake dead bird. At least Molly hoped it was fake. You never quite knew with Margot.

"We can't talk about it here. It's schmermaidy." Schmermaidy was their supersecret and completely impenetrable code word.

"Did someone see your tail?" Margot asked, weirdly serious all of a sudden.

"No," Molly said hastily. "The secret is still safe. I'm just... I've been thinking a lot about Meire. What was it like? Back in the day?"

Margot pulled a red lipstick out of her bag and started applying it to the dead bird's beak. "Poopy."

"No, like...at its prime. Before the poop."

"Oh. Less poopy."

"Margot! Please."

"I don't know, all right?" She held up the bird to admire her handiwork, looking satisfied. "You're better off asking Myla. She can probably recite the first nineteen empresses backward while hanging upside down by her tail."

Ada ambled over to their table, swinging her designer lunch box in her hand. "Hey. Wanna go and eat with the Populars?"

Molly prodded at her vol-au-vent. "Yeah, sure."

Ada's sleek bangs dropped into her eyes as she frowned. "You don't sound too thrilled. This was always the aim, right? Infiltrating their masses? Becoming at one with the Populars?"

For years, Molly and Ada had wanted to get into the popular group at school and had concocted increasingly elaborate and absurd strategies to get there. Molly had never really believed that they'd succeed, but now that Ada was dating Penalty Pete, they spent more time with the whole group than hanging out with each other.

And in reality, the Populars were quite boring. Molly sort of missed her and Ada's time as a duo, scarfing down chips in their tiny locker nook.

Molly didn't tell Ada any of this, though. Due to her afore-mentioned stubbornness, she had to keep up the pretense that being with the Populars was still hugely exciting. "No, it's cool. Let's go."

Margot glared at her in astonishment. "Rude."

"Okay," Molly said, rising to her feet. "Let's do this. Let's be bona fide Populars."

Ada did a funny little salsa dance, stamping her heels for effect. Molly laughed and copied her.

Laughing with Ada so effortlessly again felt nice. They'd had their first epic falling-out a few months ago, and they didn't speak for a long, long time. That was a particularly dark time for Molly, and it made her swear she'd never take her best friendship with Ada for granted again. She also swore she'd try to keep her hot temper under control, but that wasn't going so well. Just ask the lamppost she kicked this morning.

"Popularrrrrr," Ada crooned in a weird, high-pitched voice, making Molly laugh even harder.

Margot flexed her catapult menacingly. "For goodness' sake. The rudeness is unimaginable."

"Why don't you come too, Margot?" Ada asked, breathless from performing the impromptu Popular dance, though Molly could tell she was just being polite.

Margot snorted. "I would rather eat my own face, thanks."

"Margot," Molly interrupted. "Do you mind if I go?"

There was a split second where Molly thought her older sister might actually ask her to stick around, and if that happened, Molly absolutely would. She'd been ignoring Margot for weeks now, and she was starting to feel a little bit bad about it. Most of Margot's friends were from clamdunk, so she didn't really have many people to eat lunch with at school.

But Margot swallowed her pride and said, "Whatever. Just don't expect your bed to be entirely free of seaweed later."

Molly followed Ada to the table where the Populars were eating lunch. Penalty Pete was dribbling a piece of corn around his tray with his finger. Felicity's arm was draped possessively over Cute Steve's shoulders, which made eating her couscous very difficult indeed. Jenna and Briony, Felicity's cronies, were gossiping between themselves, giggling and whispering at something on Briony's phone.

"Hey, guys," Ada said cheerily, still a little out of breath from the Popular dance. As she sat down, the slight gleam of sweat did nothing to prevent Penalty Pete from giving her a kiss as a way of saying hello.

For a split second, Molly hovered awkwardly. The only spare seat was on the other side of Cute Steve.

"Pull up a pew," Cute Steve said pleasantly, and Molly had to fight the urge to gaze adoringly at him like he was a tall cone of glistening mint chocolate chip.

While Molly often had to help out at the family fish-and-chip shop, dressing up as a giant haddock to hand out leaflets, Cute Steve had a job at the ice-cream kiosk next door. He was very tall and very dark and very, very athletic. Molly had been in love with him since the day Minnie first learned to walk, which was not as long ago as you might have thought and had involved a pair of clumsy Rollerblades. But still.

Unfortunately, Cute Steve was going out with Molly's nemesis: Felicity Davison.

Today, Felicity pointedly did not make eye contact with Molly, which was just as well. Every time Molly was around Felicity, she felt a kind of emotional aftershock from the bizarre moment they had shared at the zoo.

It was right after Molly had abducted a penguin, and Felicity had made a comment about Molly's restaurant grease smell. A surge of world-ending anger and shame had triggered Molly's merpower for the first time, and she felt Felicity's emotions as strongly as if they were her own.

She'd relived the arguments, embarrassments, and fears that Felicity had experienced that day, including the knowledge that Felicity's mom had cancer. And Felicity knew it.

Although now, in the school cafeteria, Molly couldn't read Felicity's emotions like that—merpowers only worked while you were a mermaid—there was still a rippling wave of residual empathy. Still a connection that hadn't been there before.

It was the only time Molly had managed to use her merpower, and it had happened at exactly the right moment. She couldn't help wondering when she would next be able to tap into her mysterious gift.

As Molly sat down, Cute Steve shoveled a giant spoonful of baked beans into his divine mouth. Then he asked, "So how's it going at the restaurant?"

"Good." Molly nodded, realizing how impossible it was to eat a vol-au-vent in a seductive manner and deciding just to sip her apple juice instead. "We have a new sausage."

Cute Steve nodded his approval. "Nice."

"It's called the Edward," Molly added, a grin spreading across her face. "After my friend Eddie."

Cute Steve raised an eyebrow. "Of the Ears?"

"Exactly."

"Good guy."

Warmth tingled in Molly's chest as she thought of how Eddie had covered her shift a few weeks ago so she could go to the zoo with Ada. Despite him not having any experience in the battered-fish arena.

"OMG, have you guys heard about the new kids?" Briony asked. She had a very high voice, like a chipmunk. "There's, like, some new kids apparently."

"No way!" Ada said. Her amazement was genuine. This hardly ever happened. SPLuM was tiny, Little Marmouth was tiny, and nobody in their right mind ever moved there unless they had big dreams of becoming a chip-shop mogul and ending the Seabrooks' decades-long reign over the town's fast-food scene.

"Yep," Jenna said, nodding so hard, her topknot came loose. "Twins—a boy and a girl. Really, really athletic, apparently. Like, superhot in a totally athletic way."

"And kind of like mysterious?" Briony said. "That's what I heard anyway."

Despite the inward eye roll at Jenna and Briony's inane commentary, Molly couldn't help feeling a little bit excited. What if the girl was cool enough to rob Felicity of her queen-bee status? What if the boy was Molly's future husband? Maybe they could double-date with Penalty and Ada.

"They are real," Felicity confirmed conspiratorially. "Finn and Serena Waverley. Quite cool in, like, an obvious and completely unoriginal way. But everyone's obsessed with them." She sounded rather bitter at this last part. "Oh, there they are now!"

The volume in the cafeteria dropped about a hundred decibels as the twins walked in. Everyone with necks turned to look.

Finn and Serena Waverley were both blond, tall, and high-cheekboned—vaguely Viking looking, Molly thought. They strutted into the cafeteria with chins tilted high and charismatic grins on their symmetrical features.

To be fair to Jenna, they *were*, like, superhot in a totally athletic way.

"Fetch me my longboat," Molly whispered to Ada across the table, "for I am adrift on their tide."

"What?" Ada said.

"Vikings," Molly explained, not really explaining anything at all.

I Didn't Know There Was a Meire in West Lothian

Myla's bedroom was right at the top of Kittiwake Keep. She liked the quiet for studying, but a few weeks ago, she'd admitted to Molly that she sometimes felt hurt that nobody came to visit her up there. Molly had been making more effort ever since, bringing Myla cups of milky tea and asking what subject she was studying, even though she understood precisely none of the answers.

Considering how sensible she was, Myla was surprisingly messy. Tonight, her bed was covered in wrinkled clothes, dog-eared textbooks, and random pieces of half-eaten toast. Molly tried to clear a small corner of duvet to perch on. As she did, something tiny and furry scurried out from under a navy school sweater. Molly screamed at the top of her lungs. "A rat! A rat! It's going for your toast!"

Myla laughed and scooped the little gray fur ball up from its terrified spot on the wooden floor. "It's a rabbit. She's called Boudicca."

"Okay," said Molly after a moment. "Of course. Boudicca. Where did Boudicca come from, exactly?"

"She was queen of the Iceni people of East Anglia."

Molly fought with all her might, but her eyes rolled regardless. "I meant rabbit Boudicca."

"Ah, yes. I should've deduced that from context," Myla said in her very best Sherlock voice.

"Don't beat yourself up," Molly muttered. "Not everyone can be as intelligent as me."

"Rabbit Boudicca is a rescue. I adopted her two months ago. Nobody has noticed yet."

Molly gaped at her. "But I've been in your room lots of times in the last two months!"

"You never were that observant. Honestly, I'm surprised you didn't notice the smell."

"I did. I just thought you were too busy studying to wash your hair."

Myla smirked, stroking Boudicca absentmindedly. "That too."

With no subtle way to segue into what she really wanted to talk about, Molly plonked herself down—watching out for any other rogue mammals nesting in the chaos—and said, "Do you ever study Meire?"

"Meire?" Myla blinked. "The mermaid queendom?"

"No, Myla. Meire in West Lothian."

Myla frowned. "How interesting. I didn't know there was a Meire in West Lothian."

Molly snorted. "Myla."

"Oh. It's that sarcasm thing you do."

"Yes. I am famously the only person in the world to use sarcasm."

Myla peered disapprovingly over her thick-rimmed glasses. Boudicca purred in her lap. "I read about Meire a lot. The books beneath the trapdoor are an endless source of knowledge."

There was an ancient library hidden below the light-house, underneath the broken dishwasher. Molly remembered running a finger over those dusty tomes as though it were yesterday, although it hadn't occurred to her to revisit them. She was no good at reading long, complicated things.

Plucking at some stray crumbs on the bedsheets, Molly mumbled, "Maybe...maybe we could talk about Meire sometime. I'm not good at reading, but I'd love for you to teach me some cool stuff."

Myla grinned then, as though all her nerdy dreams had

come true at once. "I can do more than teach you about Meire. I can show you."

Heart skipping a beat, Molly asked, "What?"

"I've found a place. A little shelf of seabed from which you can just make out Balaena, the old capital of Meire." Eyes glittering with a kind of mischief Molly had never seen in her big sister, Myla added, "I have a special underwater telescope that was passed down by our ancestors."

Molly's chest was pounding with excitement now. "But won't we get in trouble? Mom doesn't like us going in the sea. And you of all people hate breaking the rules."

Then it was Myla's turn to roll her eyes. "I'm smart, Mol, not a goody-goody. That's Melissa. In fact, my curiosity often wreaks havoc with my moral compass. I'm happy to bend the rules if it means discovering something new."

Molly beamed. "You know, I really like you, Myla."

"I like you, too, kid. So, what do you say? Meire at midnight?"

Not the Kind of Place You Want to Go on Vacation

Melissa, Molly's older sister and pedantic roommate, did not like to be left out of mermaid fun. She had a record of mermaid activities that she regularly referred to, including Margot's clamdunk matches and family card nights playing snapfish, the mermaid card game. Molly suspected that if Melissa discovered she was missing out on an impromptu trip to the sea, she would not be all that happy. And yet Molly would be happy without the constant rules and lectures. She just wanted to enjoy the outing without being reminded every forty seconds about seaweed safety procedure.

Melissa fell asleep at around ten o'clock. Molly half expected to follow soon after that. She'd always been quick to drift off and often had trouble staying up late, even when there was something exciting to look forward to. Something exciting like a secret mermaid mission and catching her very first glimpse of her homeland (homesea?).

As it happened, Molly's eyes remained open, staring at the hands of the broken cuckoo clock hanging crookedly on the wall. The waves crashed against the rocks surrounding the lighthouse. The minutes inched forward as though they were moving through gooey pudding. Molly's limbs grew more and more restless. She twitched with anticipation and also with the fierce desire to transform.

Quarter to midnight eventually crawled around. Molly slipped quietly out of bed and into her fluffy slippers, which were great for muffling your footsteps. She crept down to the kitchen, where Myla was already waiting, finishing the dregs of a milky tea. Since she was nearly eighteen, Myla could stay up until whenever she wanted, and it didn't look like she'd even attempted to go to bed. She was still in the woolly green sweater and black jeans she'd been wearing several hours earlier.

Once they'd moved the broken dishwasher and descended through the trapdoor, it took Molly's eyes a few moments to adjust to the dimness in the perfectly round secret room. Slowly, the glorious sight of hundreds of dusty books materialized around her. In the brief minute before the floorboards were wound back and the sea was revealed, the only scent was that of well-loved old pages.

As they transformed—a strange, tingly feeling—Myla plucked a particularly worn tome from the shelves and laid it to one side. The gold-foiled title read *The Extremely Unauthorized but Highly Interesting Complete History of Meire*.

"You'll like that one," Myla said with a coy smile, wiggling her emerald-green tail in the spray from the gushing ripples of sea beneath them. Her long-sleeved top, which matched the color of her tail perfectly, had also materialized and glistened in the dim light.

The jumping in was the best part. Those short seconds of weightlessness as Molly dove through the air, the plunging sensation of fully immersing her body in the cool waves. The instant relief, the hit of fresh air...well, water. It never got old.

They weren't supposed to be here at all, of course. Mom was strict about when and where the Seabrook sisters were allowed to transform. They had a midnight trip down to a hidden cove once a month, where they could splash around and get it out of their system, but other than that, they were supposed to avoid transforming wherever possible. It was too dangerous, she said—too dangerous on land, because they might be seen, and too dangerous in the water, because... Actually, Molly didn't know exactly *why* it was so bad down here. All she knew was that Mom would flay her alive if she knew about the secret trips.

They swam in a different direction from Coley Cavern, where Molly went to watch Margot play clamdunk or to spy on Myla as she met her secret girlfriend. Instead, they swam farther out to sea, where the water was cooler and darker, the fish fatter and less welcoming.

On the way out, Molly was surprised to pass a few other mermaids. None of them were supposed to be this deep in the water anymore. It was too dangerous, too polluted. But they passed a group of three older mermen all carrying matching spears with octopuses carved on the stems and also a haggard old mermaid with a haunted look in her eyes.

Just as Molly was beginning to worry Myla was taking her all the way to Denmark, they stopped by a slightly raised shelf of rocky seabed. Myla perched on a jutting ledge and smiled triumphantly, pointing out into the middle of the North Sea.

Molly followed her gaze, and she saw...nothing. Just more water, more fish, more patches of light and shade. Plus, thousands and thousands of pieces of plastic garbage, from shopping bags to bottles of Coke and everything in between. The sight made her sad. Humans were awful, and they ruined everything. There was no way she'd be able to see her homeland through all that debris.

"I think you're cracking up, babe," she said kindly to Myla.

"First, I don't think our relationship can survive you calling me 'babe.' Second, be patient. Once you've seen it, you'll never unsee it."

Molly scooted over to Myla and settled down beside her. There was strangely little sensation in a mermaid tail, so sitting on rugged rocks wasn't as uncomfortable as it should have been. Molly sometimes thought she could take a bullet to the part where her kneecaps were supposed to be and not immediately notice.

Myla reached into an extremely large clamshell that had been turned into some sort of messenger bag. Molly hadn't even noticed she'd been carrying it. Inside was a dainty bronze instrument studded with pearls: the special under-water telescope she'd talked about. The word *Marefluma* was carved on the stem in ornate, swirly letters.

With eyes like fireflies in the deep blue water, Myla delicately swiveled various sections of the telescope into place. Removing her glasses, she held it up to her face and stared down its length.

"Our maternal grandmother, Murielle, passed this telescope on to Mom when Mom left Meire for the human world. Mom gave it to me when I was around your age. I was just as curious as you about Meire and its secrets. If anything, seeing this tiny glimpse has made me even more so."

She handed the telescope to Molly so carefully, you'd have thought it was a priceless diamond necklace.

"I don't think you're ready for this," Myla murmured mysteriously.

Hands trembling ever so slightly, Molly held the peculiar instrument up to her face. As soon as her eyes adjusted, she gasped.

She could see it. In blurred strokes of light and color, like the impressionist paintings Mrs. Makvandi, her art teacher, endlessly talked about.

There were swathes of copper and pearl and what she could've sworn were ancient shipwrecks. There were towering buildings in deep blue and dark green and shimmering clear glass. There were a million twinkling, moving lights swirling through the city like bees in a hive.

"Balaena," Myla announced grandly.

"What are all those lights?" whispered Molly, who had been expecting a murky ghost town. "I thought nobody lived there anymore."

Myla sat up straighter, eager to don her supergenius cap. "Once upon a time, the merministers in government paid electroreceptive fish to power the city. When the pollution got too bad for the mermaids and most of them fled to the land, the fish had nowhere to go, so they stayed in the larger towns."

"And the human government was happy to have us?" Molly asked, struggling to picture a negotiation between the two species.

"Not at first," Myla said. "In fact, the human world officials were completely unwilling to help us. But legend goes that we had a great leader representing us, and they eventually managed to make a deal. Nobody knows what we offered in return for safe refuge. But for now, we're allowed to live on land, providing we conceal our true identities. The second we slip up, we're back in the sea."

Molly mulled this over. The light through the telescope continued to shift and swirl, like the city was a living, breathing thing. "Hang on... You say most of the mermaids fled, including us. But you also mentioned our grandmother. Murielle? Where is she now? We've never met her, have we?"

"No, we've never met her."

Myla didn't meet Molly's gaze, and Molly wondered whether that was the whole truth. She reached for her merpower, trying to read Myla's emotions, but no answer came.

"Stubborn old crone, Murielle. Refused to abandon the place she'd lived her whole life, no matter how ugly things got down there. There are still a bunch of human-hating traditionalists who refuse to move to the shore."

"So, it isn't too dangerous," Molly pushed. "To live there, I mean. Or at least visit."

"I don't know about that. Rumor has it that the streets of Balaena flow with human sewage, and the mermaids who remain are forever being injured and maimed by vicious tangles of plastic. Maybe it's not as dangerous as Mom makes out, but it's still not the kind of place you want to go on vacation."

Molly's heart sank. She had a grandmother down there she'd never be able to meet. A piece of herself she'd never be able to touch.

"What else do you know about our family?" she asked, desperate for more information, for anything that would make her feel closer to her mermaid identity.

"To be honest, there are more gaps in my knowledge than I'd care to admit," Myla replied. "Mom doesn't talk about it much, about our lives back in Meire, but lately, I've been feeling like something must've happened to us down there. Something bad."

"Because we left?"

"Not just that. A lot of mermaids left. It's more... Well, why is she *so* strict about us coming down here? She only allows us in the sea when she's there to supervise. I know it's a little polluted, but how dangerous can it really be? Plus, she's accidentally let things slip to me a few times. I think there was a big fight between her and Murielle, and it's part of the reason we left Meire. I don't know, Mol. I've suspected for a while that there's a bigger reason for her fear. I just can't figure out what."

"Maybe the reason Mom never told us about the trapdoor library is because there's something in the books she wants to hide," Molly said, curiosity burning hotter than ever. "Something about our past."

Myla pressed her lips into a straight line. "If there is, I haven't found it yet."

The girls talked for a while longer until eventually, Myla suggested they head back.

On the way, Molly spotted a pair of mermaids swimming up ahead. A boy and a girl, both with long, flowing blond hair. The girl had a deep bloodred tail, and the boy's was inky black. On each of their shoulder blades was a strange, jagged scar that perfectly matched the other.

They swam playfully together, flicking shells and starfish in each other's faces. There was something vaguely familiar about them, but it wasn't until they got closer that Molly realized who they were.

Finn and Serena Waverley.

They were mermaids, too.

Ice Cream in Winter

The next day was a Saturday. A cold, gloomy winter Saturday, with the sky dark and ominous and the sea gunmetal gray. A wonderful Saturday to dress up as a haddock and hand out leaflets on a wet boardwalk, Molly was sure everyone would agree. (By everyone, she obviously meant madmen, ax murderers, and Margot, who was somewhere between the two.)

With very few passersby to harass into taking menus, Molly kept gazing out at the choppy sea. Not twelve hours earlier, she'd seen the Waverley twins swimming out there in their natural form: as mermaids. She wasn't entirely sure whether they'd seen her or not. She was equally uncertain whether it would matter if they had. After all, mermaids didn't need to keep their identities hidden from each other, just from prying humans.

Either way, the new kids in school had suddenly become a lot more interesting. For the first time in her life, Molly couldn't wait until Monday, when she'd get to see them again, if only from afar.

Thankfully, she had an entertaining way of passing the time. Eddie of the Ears was helping out on her shift. At first, he had tried to purchase a giant fish costume online, to no avail. When he asked where he could buy one, Molly had advised him that sadly, the haddock suit was an old family heirloom, and nobody was quite sure where it had come from.

So, Eddie being Eddie, he had taken to the task with aplomb and made his very own cod suit, using an ingenious combination of gray trash bags, duct tape, and strips of tinfoil cut into scales. When his mom dropped him off outside the shop and he rustled over to Molly with a dopey grin on his pale, freckly face, Molly thought her appendix might rupture from laughter. He had even donned a tinsel scarf for a festive twist.

There was nobody quite like Eddie of the Ears. And that was precisely why they'd named a sausage after him.

"You know, you really are good at being a cod," Molly said without sarcasm, for maybe the first time in her life.

"Thank you," Eddie said sincerely. "I feel very at home in this trash bag. And not at all sticky and disgusting."

"It is a grueling experience. But you get used to it."

Scratching at his stomach, he grimaced. "I have new respect for you, Molly Seabrook."

Molly clutched her hand (well, fin) to her chest in pretended offense. "You mean you didn't respect me before?"

"Not at all. You had a scrambled-egg cake for your birthday, for one thing."

Molly burst out laughing. Minnie had forgotten to include the eggs in the batter, and they'd ended up forming an omelet-like crust on top of the cake. Horrible. "You're right about that."

The problem with handing out leaflets in early December was that the boardwalk was all but abandoned for the year. As a result, Molly and Eddie had to fight to the death for customers. At one point, Eddie even tackled Molly to the ground so that he could give a flyer to a disgruntled old man ahead of her. Despite having the wind knocked out of her and a not-unheavy cod boy on top of her, Molly's sides ached from laughing.

While Eddie was still perched triumphantly on Molly, Ada appeared around the corner, bundled up in her winter coat. Climbing breathlessly to their feet, Molly and Eddie panted as though they'd just battled several Roman gladia-tors and somehow emerged victorious.

"Hey," Molly said, brushing wet dirt off her fishy behind. "Where's Pete?"

Ada rolled her eyes so hard, it caused a small earthquake. "Just take a random guess, Molly. Where on earth could Pete be on a Saturday morning?"

"Singing to the homeless? Volunteering at a soup kitchen? Washing graffiti off the city hall?"

"Close."

"He's playing soccer, isn't he?" Molly winced in sympa-thy, although Ada had known what she was getting into when she started seeing a guy called Penalty.

"Yep." Ada jingled the coins in her tracksuit pants. "Although let's be honest, I'd rather be hanging out with you guys anyway. Fish costumes or not. Want to get some ice cream? Steve looks miserable."

Little Marmouth had to be the only place in the north-ern hemisphere where they still sold ice cream in winter. Molly looked over to the kiosk for the first time all day, which was unusual. Usually, her eyes just wandered over there on their own. But with Eddie of the Ears here to distract her, she found herself not caring whether Cute Steve was looking at her.

"Excuse me," Eddie said indignantly to Ada, flicking the end of his tinsel scarf over his shoulder. "We're working here."

Ada frowned at his costume as though only just realizing that he was wearing it. "Can't you just ask Molly's mom for a break? Neither of you is getting paid."

Eddie folded his fins. "It's a matter of pride, Ada."

Ada snickered. "Is that what they call it?"

"You're just jealous that you're not dressed as a fish," Eddie said.

"Fine, fine, I'm extremely jealous and left out. Literally all I want in my life is to dress as a fish, and you two are a living reminder of this personal failure."

Eddie triumphantly held up his pointy fins as though they were pistols. "Knew it."

"But I also want ice cream." Another jingle of the coins. "Shall we?"

Two fish and a tracksuit sauntered over to the ice cream kiosk. (Molly thought this sounded like the beginning of a bad joke. Or a very strange poem.) Cute Steve looked up from his phone. If he was surprised to see the peculiar trio, he didn't show it. Maybe he was just used to Molly's very particular brand of weird.

"Hello, Steven," Molly said, just to really hammer the weirdness home.

He raised a very beautiful dark eyebrow. "Nobody has called me Steven since 2007."

"That's a shame," Molly said earnestly, trying to mirror his seriousness. "It's a lovely name."

Eddie snorted. "All right, Grandma Molly."

"Should I go get your walker?" Ada chimed in. "Maybe your knitting needles?"

Eddie hunched himself over and clutched at his back, putting on a thick Scottish accent. "Och aye the noo, who'd like a wee scone?"

Ada and Molly were beside themselves laughing, while Cute Steve simply said, "You guys are, like, fifty percent weirder outside school."

"Only fifty?" Eddie asked. "We must try harder."

There was an elderly couple nearby, stringing Christmas lights around a sad-looking fir tree. The main street was much busier than the boardwalk, with lots of people carrying shopping bags. Molly could smell the spiced-wine stall that was there all through December, and for the first year ever, she actually thought it smelled really good. Not that she'd tell her mother that.

"Are you seeing Felicity later?" Ada asked Cute Steve after he'd started scooping their ice cream. Molly found herself staring at his hands in a probably very gross way.

Why had she never noticed how nice his hands were before?

"Uh, yeah. Yep. Think so."

"I like Felicity," Molly said. "She's nice. Like mushy peas." For heaven's sake! Why did she have to describe everything in fish-and-chip-shop terms? Or comment on how much she liked his girlfriend?

Cute Steve handed Molly a cone. He'd given her an extra scoop, which in Molly's eyes was essentially a marriage proposal. "Mmm, yeah. Anyway. Oh, er. Here she is."

Molly's heart sank as she saw Felicity stroll over to them. It wasn't that she necessarily hated Felicity. Not like she used to. It was just that she always had to be a little on edge around her in case she let something slip about Molly's tail—accidentally or otherwise.

"Hey, babe." Felicity leaned over the counter and pecked Steve on the mouth. "Hey, Aydz. Hey...you guys." Her nose wrinkled at the sight—and probably smell—of Molly and Eddie in their fish costumes.

"We were just getting ice cream," Molly said, trying to keep her tone light despite the fact that her speeding pulse sounded like a malfunctioning steam engine. Every time Felicity was around, she was painfully aware of how quickly and easily her life could be ruined. She had to avoid doing anything to annoy her, and if that involved making conversation like a total simpleton, so be it.

Felicity nodded. "I see that."

Molly slurped her ice cream in an ugly way to make it very clear that she was not trying to steal Felicity's man. "Raspberry ripple."

"So, the Waverleys, huh?" Felicity said, grabbing a cake pop from the glass jar and biting into it.

"Yeah," Molly blurted out before realizing she had nothing else to add that was not secret information regarding their tail status. "Er...twins."

"Do you think they seem cool?" Ada asked as though Felicity were the oracle of coolness. "Like, should we ask them to eat lunch with us?"

"Finn plays rugby," Cute Steve said as though this settled matters. Soccer players disliked rugby players for reasons Molly could not begin to understand.

"That's true, babe," Felicity said thoughtfully. "And I think Serena is a little...*you know*..."

"Viking-y?" Molly suggested.

"Why did the Viking buy a secondhand boat?" Eddie asked. Everyone looked at him blankly. Barely containing his grin, he added, "He probably couldn't a-fjord a new one."

The appalled silence that followed was probably funnier

than the joke itself. Molly couldn't contain her laughter. She choked so violently on her ice cream cone that she thought she might get sick. Cute Steve and Felicity, who were clearly humorless beings, stared at her in bafflement.

Ada came to the rescue. "Mol, I think your mom is shouting. Should we go?"

"Oh. Okay." Molly swallowed the offending mouthful of cone. "Well, bye then."

As Molly, Ada, and Eddie wandered back to the shop, she couldn't help thinking that hanging out with the Populars wasn't all it was cracked up to be. They weren't funny or weird for a start, and the added tension with Felicity made it impossible to relax and talk like a normal human being.

It was all more hassle than it was worth. The original goal behind infiltrating the Populars was to make Cute Steve fall madly, passionately in love with her. But now that he was with Felicity, it felt a little pointless.

After Eddie's mom came to pick him up, Ada hung around and talked with Molly on the pier for a while. They discussed school and Penalty Pete and Minnie's current obsession with death metal, which she had discovered on Margot's phone.

The conversation moved from Minnie's headbanging to the Populars.

"Do you think Felicity likes me?" Ada was perched on the

windowsill of the fish-and-chip shop, shivering despite her thick coat. "Really likes me, I mean?"

"Um, I think so?" Molly said. "Why?"

"It's just...I don't know. She's seemed a little off lately." Ada's voice was soft and unsure. "I feel like I've annoyed her or something. I just hate feeling like people are angry with me, you know?"

Molly knew exactly why Felicity was off: her mom's sickness. But she couldn't tell Ada that. It was part of the pact. Even though Ada would never tell anyone, Molly couldn't break her promise without Felicity breaking hers.

All Molly knew was that she had too many secrets from her best friend, and she was getting tired of trying to keep them.

6

Something Weird about Their Faces

Monday morning at school was a tragedy of unparalleled proportions, because Melissa had been named the youngest student supervisor in SPLuM's history. And she was absolutely unbearable as a consequence.

Normally only seniors were made student supervisors, but an exception had been made for Melissa due to her "outstanding contribution to the school's moral code." This basically meant she had flattered a lot of people and was now being given a special badge as a result.

That morning, as Melissa proudly pinned the badge on her blazer in the mirror, Margot had very sincerely told her that if she dared to tattle on any of the Seabrook sisters, she would swiftly be covered in peanut butter and tied to the roof of the lighthouse for the seagulls.

Ada had choir practice at lunch, and Molly didn't want to eat with the Populars without her. She clattered her tray of kind of scary-looking spaghetti onto Margot's table. "Guess what?" she said.

Margot slurped a piece of pasta so violently, it spattered sauce all over the table. "God is real, and it is me. I am God."

"Exactly that," Molly replied. "No, I have some gossip."

She knew it was petty, but Molly was *dying* to tell someone about the Waverleys being mermaids. Myla was uninterested in gossip in all its forms. All Molly wanted was for someone to be as shocked and excited as she was.

Serendipitously, the twins chose that exact moment to enter the cafeteria. Once again, it was as though a spell descended on the school. Conversations hushed, gazes were drawn, and the temperature seemed to drop several degrees. Their presence was hypnotic. Even the Populars were completely unable to tear their eyes away from the Viking siblings.

A table of juniors and seniors all stood up at once to give the twins their seats. This was notable, because seniors and juniors at SPLuM were famous for treating younger kids with complete disdain.

Margot, on the other hand, was absentmindedly chewing her spaghetti.

"It's about Finn and Serena," Molly hissed. "My gossip. They're...*schmermaids*."

Margot looked at her like she'd just said they were fairies from Neverland. "Based on...?"

Molly swallowed, reluctant to confess the truth. Margot's revenge was almost always extreme. "I went for a swim with Myla on Friday ni—"

"Well!" Margot snapped. "Seriously."

"Yes, seriously," Molly agreed, trying to skip past it. "And I can only apologize for betraying you in such a heinous fashion. But Finn and Serena were there, I swear. Laughing and throwing starfish at each other."

Margot crunched into a piece of stale garlic bread. "I don't like them."

This surprised Molly. "Based on...?"

"I don't know," Margot said slowly. "Their faces."

"Very mature of you." Molly fought to keep her attention on her sister. She felt the magnetic lure of the twins across the room and struggled not to give in.

"No, really. There's something weird about their faces. Everything's too sharp. And their eyes... Have you ever seen eyes so pale?"

Glancing quickly at the twins' table, Molly had to admit that their eyes were striking, such a light blue they were almost white. It was unnerving. "Yeah, I guess."

Margot frowned. "They were in English this morning, and there was just...something off. The way they acted like they literally owned the place. If they really are mermaids, that's just not how we are, is it? We're supposed to lie low on the land. Stay below the radar. Not attract attention to ourselves."

At a nearby table, Melissa was loudly assigning a punishment to a sixth grader who was violating the school uniform policy with a too-short tie. While the student groaned and huffed, Melissa sounded so pleased with herself, you'd think she'd just won the Oscar for Unbelievably Irritating Tyrant.

"Melissa's dedicated to her job," Molly pointed out.

"Pfft. Yeah."

Molly studied Margot. Although her sister didn't like that many people, she didn't dislike many, either. She didn't usually have strong feelings either way. All people were just potential victims for her pranks, nothing more. So, for her to say something like this about the Waverleys was rare. "You really don't like them?"

"Maybe that's a little strong." Margot shrugged. "I just get bad vibes, that's all. It's like they don't care if they get found out."

It was possible they didn't, Molly thought. It wasn't a totally alien concept. After all, she had seen them in the sea, near the spot where you could discover Balaena.

Another thought struck Molly. If they spent a lot of time down in the deeper parts of the water flicking starfish at each other, maybe they knew more than Myla did about the true dangers of Meire. Better yet, what if the twins knew something about the Seabrooks' past? What if they knew Murielle? What if they had some kind of insight into *why* Molly's mom was so paranoid about her daughters going in the sea?

Myla seemed to think Mom was holding something back from them, but none of her research was proving useful. This might be Molly's chance to find out more. Show Myla that she could be smart too, in her own way.

Molly's stomach bubbled with excitement. She would try to get to know Finn and Serena. It would be difficult, due to her extremely low social status, but maybe she could use her new standing as a peripheral member of the Populars to trick the twins into thinking she was cool.

Of course, now that she'd realized how boring the Populars were, this would be a little bit of a chore. But still. It was worth it for the chance to find out more about Meire— and her own identity.

Ice-White Eyes

After school, all five of the Seabrook sisters convened in the kitchen for a cup of milky tea and a slice of hot buttered toast each. This was a rarity because of Melissa's extracurricular activities, Myla's intense study schedule, Mom's endless work at the chip shop, and Minnie's tendency to poop everywhere.

Rain pelted at the windows. Molly was reminded of the deliveryman who might have seen more than he should. He hadn't been back since.

"Mommy..." Minnie asked thoughtfully. She had chocolate milk instead of tea, and at least three-quarters of it was all over her shirt. "What was it like on Noah's ark?"

Mom leaned back against the stove and crunched into her toast. "How could I possibly know that?"

"Did it smell bad? From all the animal poop?"

"Minnie," Mom said patiently. "I wasn't on Noah's ark."

"But you're soooooo old." Minnie was going through a little bit of a phase in which she obsessed over how ancient her mother was.

"Not that old."

Minnie seemed to accept this, but then, "What about Adam and Eve? Do you know them?"

"Anyway," Mom interrupted. "Did much happen at school today?"

Melissa puffed out her chest. "I penalized six people for uniform violations. Honestly, how difficult is it to dress according to regulations?"

Myla pushed her glasses up her nose and sipped her tea, which steamed over her lenses. "We're still studying the Cold War, and it's been fascinating. Mr. Hackney has been teaching us all kinds of weird and wonderful facts. Did you know that the air-raid sirens used in America were so powerful that they could turn fog into rain? Oh, and the CIA undertook something called Operation Acoustic Kitty. They literally spent millions on equipping cats with spy equipment."

Margot, unsure how to top this, simply said, "I ate some garlic bread."

"I'm bored," Minnie said before skipping out of the room, humming her favorite death-metal tune.

Mom looked around at her remaining daughters with affection, cradling her mug to her flat chest. (She'd had a double mastectomy a few years ago.) "Molly? Anything notable?"

"There are some new kids," Molly replied excitedly, remembering at the last minute not to mention that they were also mermaids. She only knew that because of her forbidden trip to the sea with Myla.

Mom's eyes widened. "You haven't had new classmates for years. Who are they?"

"Finn and Serena Waverley," Margot answered darkly. "They're twins. And also mermaids."

Oh well, Molly thought. Margot had thrown herself under the bus, so she didn't have to.

"How do you know they're mermaids?" Mom asked. "And those names are familiar..."

"Overhead them whispering about Meire," Margot muttered, shooting a look at Molly. "Only explanation."

Mom shook her head in bewilderment. "I'm having the hardest time placing those names. Can you describe them to me?"

"Tall, blond, Viking-y," Molly said.

"Hmm," Mom replied. "I don't think—"

"Freakishly pale eyes," Margot interrupted. "Like, almost white. And their features are too sharp, like they've been chiseled."

Mom's mug smashed to the ground, shattering into dozens of pieces and scalding her legs with boiling tea. Melissa yelped and leaped out of the way. Myla jumped to her feet to get a towel.

Recovering quickly, Mom gasped, "I'm sorry, I'm sorry. Gosh, how silly of me. I just...ice-white eyes, you say?"

Molly was confused by her mother's reaction. "Why? What's wrong?"

Mom seemed to gather herself, grabbing a dustpan and brush and sweeping up the shards of mug. "Did you have any contact with them? Did they approach you? Try to befriend you?"

"No, but I wish they would," Molly replied. "It'd be nice to have friends who deal with the same thing we do."

Dumping the broken pieces in the trash with a dramatic crash, Mom swiveled on her heel. "Listen. I need you to do something for me, okay? I need you to stay away from those kids. Even though they probably seem very enticing and exciting, you have to keep your distance."

"Why?" Molly asked, dumbfounded. Margot looked

vaguely triumphant that Mom's reaction echoed her own instincts.

"It's hard to explain. You just have to trust me." Mom's face was pale, and her hands were trembling slightly, causing the beaded bracelets around her narrow wrists to clatter. "Please, just...be careful. All of you. Keep your distance. I mean that emotionally and literally."

"But why—"

"Enough." Mom held up her palms, signaling the end of the matter. "I won't listen to any more about this. Now go and get changed. You're needed on the Good Ship Haddock."

"What happens if Finn and Serena come in for chips?" Margot asked. "Should we hurl the deep-fat fryer at them and run screaming for the hills? Alert the police? Bury ourselves in the nearest marsh or bog?"

"Exactly," Mom said.

Molly and Myla locked eyes across the room. Myla raised an eyebrow ever so slightly as she sipped her milky tea.

She was right. Mom was definitely hiding something. And Molly was determined to figure out what.

The Nosiest Swordfish in the Ocean

That evening, Molly's shift on the Good Ship Haddock dragged. It was cold and wet, and she seriously considered calling child protection officials about her evil dictator of a mother. She had handed out precisely one leaflet. How was that worth it? Still, she did enjoy having the excuse to be terrible at school. How could she possibly do all her homework when she spent half her life haddocking? All right, so Melissa and Myla managed it, but they were freaks of nature who actually understood the subjects they were studying.

Molly spent the whole shift half praying the Waverleys would walk around the corner and half dreading it. Margot had heard they lived on Second Street, only a few blocks away, and Molly thought it was statistically likely that if they'd only just moved in, they might be looking for takeout for dinner.

Part of her wanted them to find the chip shop. It would give her the perfect opportunity to get to know them outside school and build up some name and face recognition.

It seemed to Molly that figuring out why Mom had issues with the Waverleys was the start of unraveling whatever else she was hiding: about the sea, about Meire, and about the Seabrooks' past.

On the other hand, Finn and Serena seeing her in a haddock suit would probably eliminate any and all cool points Molly had managed to accumulate. And she had not managed to accumulate very many.

In any case, it was probably for the best that they didn't show up. Because of the stormy winter tide crashing against the boardwalk, Molly kept accidentally transforming into a mermaid and having to drag herself over to the shop to switch back. In the end, she got so fed up with bruised hips and scraped palms that she pinned herself against the shop window like a soggy Christmas display. (She had taken to wearing a tinsel scarf, too. Eddie of the Ears was nothing if not a trendsetter.)

At school the next day, Molly still felt cold and damp to her bones. She had to keep pulling her sweater sleeves down over her hands to hide her scraped palms and faint tinge of frostbite. Tonight would be the night she put her foot (well, tail) down with her mother and refuse to work until spring tourist season began. She'd argue that she could use all her new spare time to catch up on schoolwork when really she'd hide out at Ada's, watching old Disney movies and eating her body weight in Pringles.

By midmorning, a rumor had spread like wildfire that the Waverleys were having an end-of-semester party. School was buzzing with the thrill of it. Molly could almost feel the crackle in the hallways, the heat of desperation among everyone who wanted an invitation.

Tragically, Molly was one of the desperate. If she could get an invitation to the party of the century—apparently they were hiring tiger cubs to serve the Christmas pudding—then she could work her way from acquaintance of the Populars to a real friend. After that, she could reveal to the Waverleys that she, too, was a mermaid, start asking some of the questions she was dying to know the answers to, and finally figure out why Mom was being so weird about them.

At lunchtime, Ada had orchestra practice, because she was one of those wholesome types with about five thousand hobbies, while Eddie of the Ears was tutoring the same fifth-grade kid he'd tutored all semester. This meant it was just Molly and Margot, as usual. Molly was really growing to like their lunch dates. Even if she did usually wind up with grapes shoved into her nose and the stench of stink bombs on her blazer.

Today was lasagna day, which was one of the better days because of the melted cheese. As Molly began eating, she looked up at her sister and said, "Do you know, I think I'd really like school if it weren't for all the classes."

Margot smirked. "So, lunch. You like lunch."

"Lunch with my favorite sister," Molly said with a beam, displaying a mouthful of tomatoey pasta. She knew Margot would see right through it.

As suspected, Margot rolled her eyes. "What do you want?"

"To talk about Mom's reaction to Finn and Serena."

"Knew it. I mean, it *was* pretty wild. But still. What's your fixation with them?"

Molly shrugged. "Look, it's just... You have your clamdunk friends, and Myla has Amy. I really want some mermaid friends of my own, you know?"

"Yeah," said Margot. "I get it. Just doesn't seem like it should be the Waverleys. Mom seemed pretty against them."

"But *why*?" Molly asked, fully aware that she sounded a little whiny. "Why do you think Mom reacted so badly? How do you think she knows them?"

"Maybe from Meire?" Margot's top button was undone, as usual, but the teachers had pretty much given up on Margot

Seabrook, and Melissa was forbidden from disciplining her own flesh and blood.

"But Mom left before we were born," Molly said, remembering what Myla had said about Murielle. "Which means she left before Finn and Serena were born, too. Unless she had a beef with their parents—"

"I think you mean a *trout* with their parents," Margot corrected.

"Yes. Sorry." Instead of "what's your beef?" the Seabrook sisters had always asked each other "what's your trout?" because of their inherent fishiness.

Margot sipped her soda. "You want to find out more, don't you?"

"You don't? You're normally the nosiest swordfish in the ocean."

"First, very good metaphor. Shakespeare would approve. Second, did you know Shakespeare was a merman?"

Molly couldn't tell whether she was joking. "Umm, okay."

"It's literally in his name, Molly. He was famous for shaking his spear."

Molly eyed Margot with interest. Her sister was being extremely evasive, which wasn't normally her style. She was as direct as a dart to the head. When Margot was being evasive, it meant she had something to hide.

Laying down her fork, Molly folded her arms. "Do you know something I don't?"

"I know many things you don't," Margot said vaguely.

"Did you already know Finn and Serena were mermaids before I told you?"

"What?" Ada asked.

Molly's blood froze. Ada was standing right next to them, clutching her tuba and her packed-lunch box. Very much not in orchestra practice.

How much had she heard? They were supposed to be much more careful than this in public places. It was all Molly's fault. Margot had tried to shut down the conversation, and she'd persevered anyway.

"Ada," Molly said weakly. "How come you're not...?"

Ada's expression was a mixture of confusion and mirth. "It was canceled. Miss Palmer has the flu. What did you just say? Something about mermaids?"

Molly's mind went blank. "Er—"

"It's a new insult," Margot said, so nonchalantly that even Molly believed her. "All over Instagram. Means someone's shallow and arrogant and...scaly. Standard mermaid qualities, you know."

Ada frowned, still not sitting down. "I don't remember Ariel being like that."

"Well, she was," Margot said. "Stuck-up cow." She didn't seem to be anywhere near as spooked as Molly, but it was possible she was just a much better actress.

"Want to go and eat with Pete and the gang?" Ada asked Molly.

Molly was about to turn down the offer because of Margot's murderous expression, but when she looked over to the Populars' table, she noticed that the Waverleys were at the next table over and seemed to be chatting to Felicity, Briony, and Jenna.

This was it. Her first chance to get close to them...and potentially secure her invite to the party.

"Molly," Margot warned. "Careful."

Molly smiled pleasantly. "Yup. Will do."

As they got closer and closer to the Populars' table, Molly felt the Waverleys' lure growing in strength, and she had to force herself not to sprint over there. For some reason, knowing she wasn't supposed to talk to them made it all the more thrilling. They were forbidden fruit, and Molly wanted to gorge on them.

Ada sat down next to Penalty Pete, commencing the inevitable kiss, while Molly managed to sit next to her for once. This was good, because it meant she was facing the Waverleys' table rather than having her back turned to it.

Finn and Cute Steve were halfway through a lively rugby-soccer debate while Serena was mid-conversation with Felicity, pale eyes glittering like icicles under the harsh cafeteria lighting. "You're so much cooler than the girls in our last school. Honestly, all they cared about was makeup and boys."

Felicity blushed. "Yeah. Makeup and boys are so boring."

Molly knew for a fact that Felicity enjoyed both of those things, but she couldn't really blame her for lying. She would probably do the same if it made Serena like her.

"So, what's cool to do in Little Marmouth?" Serena asked, nibbling at a tuna sandwich.

"The arcade on the boardwalk is fun," Jenna said quickly, words tumbling out like marbles. "Like, in an ironic way," she added as though suddenly doubting her suggestion.

"Cool," Serena said, smiling kindly. "Maybe you can show me sometime?"

Jenna beamed in delight. Briony looked absolutely furious, whether at Serena for threatening to steal her best friend or at Jenna for managing to get Serena's attention. Molly would be lying if she said she wasn't a little jealous too.

Serena's piercing gaze flicked up to Molly. She smiled. Molly noticed her pearly teeth were a little pointed at the tips, like those of a shark. "Hey. I'm Serena."

Molly felt her cheeks burn for no good reason. "Oh. Um.

Hey. I'm Molly. Molly Seabrook. My family has the fish-and-chip shop on the pier. Just if you're going to the arcade. It's, like, next door."

"Awesome," Serena said, smiling again. "I love fish and chips."

"Me too," said Felicity passionately, as though she hadn't spent most of middle school mocking Molly for her family business. "Do you like ice cream, Serena? My boyfriend works at the *best* kiosk."

The conversation swiftly moved on without Molly, but she basked in the glow of Serena's warm comment for the rest of the day. So much so that she forgot about Ada overhearing the mermaid conversation with Margot.

Hours later, when she finally remembered, she realized she'd been a little ridiculous to get that worked up. After all, Ada would never think mermaids were actually real just from one overheard remark. Would she? No. Unless she saw a tail with her own two eyes, the secret was safe for now.

Little did Molly know, the worst was yet to come.

CHAPTER
9

A Playdate with a Noodlefish

The next morning, Molly decided it was the right time to talk to her mother about how unfair she thought it was that she should have to work outside in the bitter cold while all her classmates were getting excited for Christmas from the comfort of their warm homes.

After everyone else had left for school—Melissa always set off early to walk Minnie to her school—Molly hung back for a few moments, pretending to check her homework and make sure she'd packed everything. Mom was frowning over some tax paperwork, looking perturbed by the figures. Not looking at her mug, she kept trying to pick up her coffee with her spare hand but missing the handle every time.

Taking a deep breath to steady herself, Molly leaned

against the eggplant-colored stove. "Mom, there's something I want to talk to you about."

Her mother didn't even look up, though she did finally make contact with her coffee mug, her chunky gold rings clinking against the handle. "Mmm?"

"Mom," Molly said, irritation prickling under her skin already. "Are you listening?"

"What? Yes. Sorry, sweetheart." Mom still seemed distracted, but at least she was meeting Molly's eye now. "What is it?"

"I don't want to dress as a haddock anymore," Molly said, fighting hard to keep the wobble out of her voice. She didn't know why she felt like such a child, but she didn't want any tears to confirm her immaturity. She wanted to show she could hold an adult conversation without getting upset or losing her temper. "I mean, not *never*. I like it in the summer." The word *like* was a little strong, but Molly wanted to keep Mom on her side. "But it's so horrible and cold in the winter. And with the tide always so high and stormy, I keep transforming all the time."

Mom didn't seem surprised by this. She looked out the window at the gray, drizzly sky. "Well, you're not old enough to work in the shop. And it's not fair for you not to have to work while Myla, Margot, and Melissa do."

The second she realized this wasn't going her way, Molly's emotions threatened to take over. All she wanted to do was stomp her foot and storm out, but that wouldn't get her anywhere. She needed to stay rational and counter her mom's points with facts.

Come on, Molly told herself. *Stand your ground. You're thirteen now. You're practically an adult. She has no right to tell you what to do.*

She folded her arms firmly. "It's also not fair to catch frostbite."

"That's true," Mom conceded. "I suppose it might be hard to hand out fliers without fingers." She glanced down at her tax paperwork again. "I'll tell you what. When it's dry outside, you can still tend the Good Ship Haddock, but when it's wet and miserable, you can do some deep cleaning in the shop. Maybe even put up some Christmas decorations. And I think maybe we could find some allowance for you in return. What do you think?"

As far as compromises went, this seemed like a pretty good one to Molly. She gave her mom a huge hug, muttered "love you," and headed out to school. However, the victory felt hollow as she traipsed through the drizzle to SPLuM.

At first, she couldn't figure out why. Things were progressing with the Waverleys, and she'd (sort of) gotten her way with the endless haddocking. She was getting along well with her sisters at the moment, and Eddie was making her laugh on an almost secondly basis. She was even starting to enjoy the fact that she was a mermaid, especially sharing this hidden identity with the coolest kids in school.

Then she figured it out. Her low mood was because of Ada and the secrets she was being forced to keep from her best friend of so, so many years. Ada had no idea who Molly really was. It was an awful thing to think about. How would she feel if Ada was keeping such an enormous secret from her? She was desperate to talk about all the nitty-gritty of mermaid life: the broken dishwasher leading to the mermaid library, Myla's mermaid girlfriend, the glittering city of Balaena and how badly she wanted to visit (plus the poop-shaped reason she couldn't).

Molly realized that the reason her heart had been pounding so badly during yesterday's close call—when Ada overheard her talking about Finn and Serena's hidden identities—was that deep down, she *wanted* her best friend to find out. But it was simply too dangerous to tell her. Even though she trusted Ada with her life and knew she'd never expose Molly on purpose, everyone made mistakes. There was no guarantee Ada wouldn't slip up at some point.

No, she'd just have to focus on her mission to get closer

to the Waverleys. Then she'd finally have people in school she could share her mermaid life with.

ℓ·ℓ·ℓ

Throughout the morning, Molly's attempts to make contact with the twins were thwarted at every corner. In the hallways, they were always surrounded by people, and at lunch, they were nowhere to be seen. Some people said they'd been whisked off to take some tests to figure out which classes they should be put in for each subject, while others insisted they'd had an invitation to afternoon tea from the Duchess of Cambridge herself. There was really no way of knowing which was true.

In the afternoon, Molly had field hockey, because PE teachers loved nothing more than giving hypothermia to the children they supervised. Molly's fake migraine did not work, so she found herself playing sweeper, right in the firing line of Elsa Mitchell, SPLuM's finest center striker. The goalie yelled at Molly every time she ducked out of the way of the ball instead of trying to tackle Elsa. Ada, who was playing midfield on Molly's side, found this absolutely hilarious and dropped back just to watch her best friend's humiliation. Then Ada also got in trouble for accidentally holding her hockey stick upside down for over five minutes without noticing. The only sport either of them were any good at was chip eating.

That night, Margot had an important game of clamdunk—the famous mermaid sport—that she simply couldn't miss. Clamdunk was both very simple and very complicated. Like a halfway house between lacrosse and water polo, teams of mermaids hurled a giant pearl around with fishing nets, trying to toss it into the opposition's clam-shaped goal. It made perfect sense...until you tried to figure out the scoreboard.

Molly always had trouble remembering the rules, because they were convoluted. There were twelve players per team: one keeper, nine chalkers, and two hawkers. The chalkers focused on scoring goals—ten points per clamdunk. That part was easy enough. Meanwhile, the hawkers scooted around stealing tiny pearls, called pearlilles, from their opponents. Once a pearlille was "snatched," it was gone for the whole game, the player had to leave the pitch, and their team lost ten points. The game only ended once every chalker on a team had lost their pearlille.

The winner was the team with the highest score once the game was over, which was usually the team with their pearlilles still intact. *Usually.*

Margot, who played as a chalker, was extremely good because of her superstrength, which propelled her through the water faster than anyone else. She was the youngest player in the Northern League's history.

Unfortunately, tonight's match was an away game, and their mom (who didn't know Margot played, let alone regularly snuck out for team practice) had really been clamping down on any and all trips to the sea. Whoever the Waverleys really were, their arrival in Little Marmouth had truly shaken her, to the point where she was threatening to hang Molly and her sisters from the ceiling by their tails if they dared enter the water unsupervised. The sooner Molly and Myla could figure out the reason behind her paranoia, the better.

In any case, Melissa refused to come with them to the match. Even though she'd snuck out with them before, Mom's warnings had never been so severe. Molly suspected the whole student supervisor thing was getting to her head. She'd caught Melissa polishing her badge with chip grease behind the shop counter when she thought nobody was looking.

The Marmouth Marlins, Margot's team, were playing against the Toptyne Tunas, whose home pitch was a good sixty miles down the coast. Apparently, Margot's coach had hired a fleet of stingrays to transport the team down from Coley Cavern (which Molly thought sounded like a perfectly sane and reasonable way to travel). All Margot and Molly had to do was sneak out of the lighthouse at around ten p.m. and make it to the cavern unseen. But considering Mom's bedtime was usually well after that, there were going to be some issues.

However, prank queen Margot had it all in hand. At around nine thirty, she would sneak up to Minnie's bedroom and place her chubby fingers in a bowl of warm water. ("Not overly original," Margot acknowledged, "but sometimes simple is best.") Within ten minutes, Minnie would wake up crying for her mom, like she always did when she wet the bed, and Molly and Margot could use the diversion to sneak out through the trapdoor. Myla was primed to push the broken dishwasher back over the trapdoor before Mom returned.

At first, everything went smoothly. Minnie didn't wake up when her hand was put in the water, then Margot and Molly hid in the downstairs bathroom so they wouldn't pass Mom on the staircase as she dashed up. The inevitable wails came ten minutes later, and a sighing Mom headed up to tend to her youngest. The coast was clear, and the two girls snuck out of the bathroom and into the kitchen to meet Myla. Working quickly and silently, Margot moved the broken dishwasher into the middle of the kitchen and grabbed the handle on the top of the trapdoor.

That was where it all started to go wrong.

The second Margot yanked upward, a siren started to blare. A loud, piercing wail, like a burglar alarm crossed with a wounded jungle cat. Margot dropped the trapdoor in shock and horror. The wailing stopped immediately, but it was too late.

Mom's hurried footsteps sounded on the stairs. Before Molly and Margot could hide, she appeared in the doorway with an absolutely livid look on her face. She looked as though she wanted to scream and shout and was only just managing to restrain herself because of the two-fifths of her children asleep upstairs. "What on earth do you think—"

"We were just...er..." Margot trailed off, clearly still stunned by the installation of an alarm on her trusty trapdoor.

"Don't bother," Mom hissed, holding up a shaking palm. Her skin had gone sheer white from rage. "Just do not bother with the excuses. Do you think I'm some kind of idiot? I am furious, girls, and I would love to say I expect better from you, but...well, I don't. Hence the alarm. How could you... Myla, I *did* expect better from you. How could you let—"

"She tried to stop us," Molly interjected, feeling enormously guilty over the panic on Myla's face. Her wonderful older sister was so unused to being told off that Molly wasn't sure she could handle it without an immediate physical breakdown.

"Very well," Mom muttered. "Where on earth were you going at this hour?"

Margot smirked like she always did when she was in trouble. It was a serious character flaw, because it almost never disarmed anyone's anger. "Molly has a playdate with a noodlefish."

Mom's eyes bulged with anger. "Margot, this is not the time!"

"Fine," Molly said, taking matters into her own hands. She decided to tell a half-truth. "We've just been craving it, all right? You know that horrible on-edge feeling you get when you haven't been in the water for a while? Like your bones are unsettled? We're both just...pent-up. We needed to get out. Let off some steam. We were only going for a quick dip to get it out of our systems."

Mom looked surprised by Molly being so straight with her. It brought some of the color back to her cheeks. "I understand that. I do. But it's not safe. And really, sneaking around is not the answer. You could've gotten in real trouble. What if something happened to you? And nobody knew where you were? I can't even... Anyway, you're both grounded for the next week."

As Molly and Margot traipsed upstairs, Molly whispered, "We're trying it again, right?"

"Yup," Margot replied without hesitation. "Meet me in my room in ten."

A Stingray Named Paul

Margot and Minnie had their own teeny rooms on the first floor. Melissa and Molly shared a medium room on the second, next to the bathroom, while Mom was on the third, and Myla was on the fourth. It was a very tall and wonky lighthouse, with a sweeping spiral staircase rising through the middle. Wearing her very fluffiest slippers to muffle her footsteps, Molly waited nine minutes, trying to control her shallow breathing so as not to wake Melissa, then snuck down to Margot's room.

After their secret knock—one long one, three short ones, and another long one—Molly crept into Margot's room. Margot was sitting cross-legged on the bed, unraveling what appeared to be a rope ladder. The window was wide open.

A pit of dread gaped open in Molly's stomach. "We're not

actually climbing out the window, are we?" She wasn't scared of heights. It was just that no sane person could possibly not hate them.

"You don't have to." Margot shrugged. "I am. My team needs me."

"Yes, but we also need you. Like, alive."

"Heartwarming. Help me tie this, would you?" Margot shook out the rope ladder, which was full of knots and kinks and an alarming quantity of frays, and started attaching it to her bedposts. "If you don't do it correctly, I'll break all my limbs and probably my neck."

"Fantastic."

They worked quickly, and Molly triple- and quadruple-checked the knots to make sure they were secure. She couldn't be totally sure, seeing that she was not a sailor, but they looked pretty sturdy.

Without even a second of hesitation, Margot climbed onto the windowsill and positioned herself for the descent. "You coming?"

Molly got the impression this was not Margot's first rodeo.

This was a bad idea. This was dangerous and risky and really, really not worth it just to watch her sister lob a pearl around a large stretch of water for a while. But Molly was still angry with her mom for being weird about the Waverleys, for installing an alarm, for grounding them. The anger fueled her to do something, even if that something was very stupid indeed.

"Yup. I'm coming."

Somehow, they both made it down to the front yard unscathed, then snuck stealthily over the wall and onto the other side of the pier. From there, they were able to drop straight into the sea, although it was a much more seaweedy, foamy entrance than the one they were used to beneath the lighthouse. Molly spluttered as she swallowed a mouthful of brown slime on the way in.

Once they were fully submerged, Margot was on a mission. Knowing how late they were, she took off in the direction of Coley Cavern at such an absurd speed that Molly was left floundering in her wake. Soon, Margot was just a blob in the distance, so Molly had to find her way to the cavern from memory alone. Which was hard, because most water looks the same.

Still, she reached what looked like an underwater cliff, which she knew to be the entrance to the cavern. The wall of rock had a small, diamond-shaped opening that Molly squeezed through into another, warmer body of water. Then she propelled herself directly upward until she broke through the surface.

The cavern was empty. Margot was treading water a few feet away, looking devastated. "They left without me."

"Margot, I'm so sorry."

"We're not that late." Margot's voice was hollow and echoey, bouncing off the rugged walls of the cavern.

"Maybe you could still make it if you swam?" Molly suggested. She still had the taste of brown slime in her mouth and was trying very hard not to gag. "You're so fast."

Margot looked uncertain, which was an absolute rarity. "Sixty miles is so...far."

"Yeah, but it only took you about thirty seconds to get here from the lighthouse, and it's what, one mile? And you know the way, right? It's just straight down the coast until you get to the dancing tuna statue."

Margot considered it, then turned away. Her winged eyeliner was all smudgy from the water. "I'll still miss the beginning. There's no point."

"But you might make the second half," Molly insisted, unsure why she was pushing this so hard. Maybe because she knew how much it meant to Margot and was annoyed that Mom's paranoia was getting in the way of her sister's happiness. "And even if you miss the whole thing, you can still explain to your coach what happened. And show some support for your teammates. That way, they won't be mad at you for not showing up."

Margot opened her mouth, gathered a load of water,

then spat it up in the air like a water fountain. It went all over her own face, and she seemed genuinely surprised at this outcome. "Okay. But only if you come with me."

"Me?" Molly asked in surprise. "I'll slow us down. I can't swim half as fast as you."

Margot bit her bottom lip. "I don't want to go alone. The sea scares me a little, all right?"

Molly laughed. Not because it was funny but because it was so unexpected. "What are you talking about? You've always been the first person to suggest a sneak-out swim."

"Only in the cavern, where I know it's safe." Margot looked deeply uncomfortable at this confession of vulnerability. "The stories about the deep sea and Meire... I don't like it, Molly. What if I get caught in some old fishing nets and there's no one there to help me out? I'd drown. Well, starve to death. Since I have gills and all. There's only so much plankton a girl can eat."

Molly grinned, fighting the urge to squeeze Margot's hand underwater. Her sister liked affection as much as she liked the dentist, which, judging by the fact that she'd once punched the dentist in the face for suggesting a filling, was not very much. "Okay. I'll come with you."

What the heck. She'd come this far.

Although their mermaid vision allowed them to see

underwater, for some reason, it felt darker and colder down the coast, as though the farther they got from home, the more light and warmth they lost. Molly's muscles were burning with the effort of trying to keep up with Margot, who kept looking over her shoulder every twenty seconds as if to say, "What's taking you so long?"

To be fair, there was an awful lot of plastic and other trash in the sea. Molly was almost knocked out by a two-liter bottle of soda, while Margot got her tail tangled in an old fruit crate. If it was this bad by the shore, how awful must Meire be? Molly had second thoughts about her burning desire to visit.

After half an hour, Molly was really starting to regret her decision, but they must have been nearly halfway by then. It would have been just as much effort to turn around and go back. Still, her heart thudded in her chest, and her tail ached like never before.

As they rounded a jutting corner in the coastline, however, Molly saw the last thing she expected to see.

The Waverley twins, riding a stingray in the direction of the dancing tuna.

They were around thirty yards away and hadn't spotted the Seabrooks yet. It looked like they'd stopped to untangle some plastic straws from Serena's hair.

Molly's heart surged with excitement. This was it! If she

could reveal herself as a fellow mermaid, she would *definitely* have an in with the most popular twins in school. She grinned and turned to her sister.

Margot's reaction was the exact opposite to Molly's.

"Oh no. We should go back," Margot groaned.

"No!" Molly said at once, inspiration striking. "Let's ask them for a ride." Not only could she start laying the groundwork to becoming friends with the twins, she could also spend the journey probing for more information about Meire and hopefully get a little closer to figuring out why Mom was being so strict.

Margot whipped around to face Molly so fast, she almost snapped her neck. "Are you for real? Mom would literally murder us if she found out."

"There's a good chance that's going to happen anyway. Come on. My muscles are killing me. I'm not sure how much farther I can swim."

Margot sighed in defeat. "If someone had told me a year ago that you'd be the one getting me in trouble..."

The girls hurried to catch up to the Waverleys' stingray. As they closed in, Molly once again spotted those peculiar symmetrical scars on their shoulder blades—jagged, white, and slightly raised.

Turning to face them, Serena clutched her hand to her

chest. "Molly! Oh my gosh, you're a mermaid?" She turned to Margot and gasped. "You're Margot Seabrook!"

Margot folded her arms warily. Molly had forgotten her sister's total disdain for the Waverleys, outside her belief that fraternizing with them would lead to being murdered by their own mother. "Uh, yes. I am," Margot said. "We're in the same IT class."

"No, like *Margot Seabrook*." The weight Serena put on the name was like she was announcing the prime minister of Uzbekistan. "Chalker for the Marmouth Marlins."

"We didn't put two and two together," Finn said reverently. "This is so cool."

Molly realized they were both wearing green Marlins jerseys. They were obviously big clamdunk fans, hence big Margot fans. This could not have worked out any better.

"But wait, aren't you late for the match?" Serena asked, looking down at a strange watch on her wrist. It seemed to have moons instead of numbers.

"Yup," Molly chipped in, eager to get into the conversation. "Super late. We missed the stingray transport and are now foolishly swimming sixty miles so she doesn't miss it."

Margot looked over at Molly like she might strangle her with a squid's tentacle.

"Oh gosh, you poor things!" Serena gushed. "Here, hop

on Paul." She gestured to the stingray. "There's plenty of room."

Molly thought a stingray named Paul was possibly the funniest thing she'd ever heard in her life.

That Strange Glow

Despite his inherently sting-y nature, riding Paul was much more pleasant than swimming.

At first, Molly focused on chatting with the twins about school—what they thought of the teachers, what their favorite subjects were, that kind of thing. Her heart skipped once or twice when Finn compared SPLuM to their old schools down in Meire. Apparently, the Waverleys had only moved up to the land a few years ago, when the pollution got too bad even for their human-hating mother to cope with.

Molly buzzed with excitement. If she wanted to find out more about Meire, the Waverleys were the key. And this little jaunt by their sides was great for jimmying the lock.

Margot stayed stubbornly silent most of the way, so Serena eventually gave up asking her questions about how she'd gotten into clamdunk and chatted with Molly instead. They talked about how the Seabrook sisters were only half mermaid and about Molly's reaction when she found out on her thirteenth birthday. Finn found Molly's impression of her past self trying to crawl up the beach hilarious. Bolstered by their friendliness, Molly was about to ask them if they knew any Seabrooks down in Meire when they arrived at the dancing tuna statue. As the Waverleys paid Paul with some peculiar coinage, Molly had to fight to keep her disappointment under control.

Would she get another chance to ask her questions?

Yes. She'd just have to secure a party invite.

From the statue, the four of them swam quickly into the mouth of a river—it was tough swimming against the current, although Margot seemed to have no issue with it—and took a sharp left into a well-concealed underwater cove. Nearby was a tiny opening, covered by a giant clam-shaped stone, which also had the dancing tuna engraved on it. They pushed it to one side, swam sharply upward, and broke through the surface of the water. As they did, the roar of an ongoing match met them.

They'd made it. Barely.

The Toptyne Tunas' pitch was very similar to Coley Cavern. The cavern was strung with thousands of twinkling lights, and seashell ropes hung around the pitch, which was a large pool in the middle of the cove with a clam-shaped goal at either end.

DON'T TELL HIM I'M A MERMAID

Hundreds of merfolk with a dazzling rainbow array of tails perched on jutting rocks around the water. The game was well under way, a blur of green and blue jerseys hurtling up and down the pitch, and the clamor in the cavern was deafening.

One glance at the scoreboard showed the Marlins were down 170–40. Without their secret weapon, it was no surprise, but it didn't make a warm reception from her teammates any more likely. Molly's stomach twinged with discomfort for her sister.

Margot's coach was swimming unhappily up and down the side of the pitch. The elderly mermaid was stern, with a permanently furrowed brow. Margot cringed at the sight of her. "Time to face the music."

"I'll see you after?" Molly said. "I'll wait with Serena and Finn. We'll find a spot and watch you kick butt."

"If I'm ever allowed on the pitch again," Margot grumbled, setting off dejectedly in the direction of her coach.

Looking around, Molly thought her promise to get a good spot was an empty one. The cavern was packed tight, and there wasn't a spare perch in sight.

Serena shrugged. "Leave it to us." She sashayed over to the nearest spot to the pitch, batted her eyelashes at two older mermaids, and said, "Do you mind if we sit here?"

If Molly had tried such a move, she'd undoubtedly have

been laughed out of the sea. But there was something ethereal about Serena's manner. She almost...*glowed* as she asked, and in a not entirely natural way. Her skin grew luminous, and her pale eyes gleamed even whiter, like fresh pearls. Her voice sang, the words rippling and dancing in the echoey cavern.

Instantly, the two mermaids leaped up as though they'd been stung by jellyfish, gesturing for the twins to take their place. Finn smiled smugly at Molly, and the three of them shimmied up onto the rock. The displaced mermaids looked confused, as though they didn't quite understand what had just happened.

Something about the exchange unsettled Molly. The way the other mermaids hadn't even put up a fight, hadn't asked any questions. And that strange glow... She'd seen the hypnotic effect Finn and Serena had on the kids in school, but this was a whole new level.

"So, Molly, you live in the lighthouse on the pier, right?" Finn asked, picking a piece of seaweed off his inky black tail. Molly noticed he had the same slightly pointy teeth as Serena.

"Yeah," Molly said, surprised. "How did you know?"

"Oh, we were just exploring the town last night and saw you walking home," he said. "How long have you lived there? Do you have any other brothers or sisters?"

"Finn!" Serena laughed, though a little tensely. "Too many questions."

"Sorry," Finn said. "I'm just curious. There were no other merfolk in our last town, so this is a novelty. Do you go down to the sea much?"

"Not really," Molly admitted. "Mainly we just sneak out for clamdunk."

"Sneak out?" Serena asked in surprise. "Your mom doesn't let you go in the sea?"

"Only if she's there to supervise. It's weird."

Serena and Finn exchanged an unreadable expression. It sent a jolt of anticipation through Molly's veins. Did they know something she didn't? From the secretive looks on their faces, it didn't seem like something they wanted to share.

Maybe she could use her merpower to read their minds, like she had Felicity's.

Not really remembering *how* exactly she'd done it before, she focused very, very hard on the twins. She pictured herself rummaging through their brains like at a yard sale, trying to find the thoughts she wanted. She concentrated so hard that it gave her a little bit of a headache.

Nothing happened. There was no hot surge like there had been at the zoo, no wave of easy-to-decipher emotions rolling off the Waverleys. She would have to try and get as much out of them through normal conversation as she could.

Just as Molly was about to ask whether Finn and Serena's

parents were equally strict, there was a booming cheer as a substitute was announced: Margot Seabrook. The twins went wilder than anyone else. Molly realized they really were fans of her sister.

Margot scored a screamer of a dunk. From that moment on, Molly was too engrossed in the match to keep probing the Waverleys. Margot's presence on the pitch lifted the Marlins' spirits, and they began to stage a remarkable comeback, even though half their players had already been snatched. The atmosphere in the cavern transformed from the discomfort of watching a humiliating defeat to the excitement of realizing you might be witnessing something really special.

In the end, the mountain was too high to climb, and the Toptyne Tunas finally claimed the victory by stealing Margot's pearlille. But the Marlins' coach looked significantly less humiliated than she had when they arrived, and as Margot was gathered up in a group hug by her teammates, Molly figured she was off the hook. Everyone had forgiven her.

Apart from their mother, of course. Molly dreaded to think what wrath was waiting for them when they got back to Kittiwake Keep.

A Herd of Goats in Mumbai

As it happened, Myla had been the ultimate team player and prevented their mom from discovering that they'd snuck out for a second time. She'd seen the rope ladder drop past the living-room window, made sure Mom was safely in the kitchen, then dashed upstairs to pull the rope ladder back up before anyone was the wiser. She then stayed up studying until the wee hours of the morning so she could keep an eye out for Molly and Margot's return, at which point she and Boudicca welcomed them quietly in through the front door. Mom had long since gone to bed.

They seemed to have gotten away with the entire plan. You know, apart from already being grounded. That was mildly inconvenient.

In any case, Myla was skyrocketing through the rankings

as one of Molly's favorite sisters. Margot really had to up her game if she wanted to retain her top spot.

The next morning, Mom barely said two words over breakfast, which was fine by Molly and Margot because of their severe tiredness. They hadn't gotten back to bed until after two in the morning, having hitched a stingray ride back to Coley Cavern with the rest of the team, and Molly's school alarm went off at six thirty. Margot was so sleepy at the kitchen table that she poured orange juice over her Cocoa Krispies (and said it was actually quite tasty in a chocolate-orangey kind of way).

The whole morning, Molly's eyes stung with exhaustion. The combination of salt and lack of sleep made her feel like her pupils would spontaneously combust if she didn't close them immediately. Both math and science absolutely dragged, to the point where Molly genuinely thought Ms. Stavros might be some sort of witchy Time Lord who had enchanted the clocks into crawling backward.

Thankfully, Eddie of the Ears took a break from being a model student to try and keep Molly entertained and awake. He turned everything their chemistry teacher said into a funny little rap song, which Molly was pretty sure he could sell to the exam board for a significant sum.

Because she was tired and not paying as much attention

as she should, there were a few close calls in terms of sponta-neous transformations. Walking past the swimming pool on her way to the art department, she almost forgot to give the building a wide-enough berth, and only the tingling in her kneecaps caused her to leap out of the way just in time. This did not look particularly normal or smooth to Ada and Eddie, who looked at her like she had some kind of rare jack-in-the-box disease.

Then there was the soggy puddle in the entrance hall, formed by hundreds of rain-soaked shoes clomping across the tile. It was big enough to cause a transformation, and Molly had to do a sort of sprint and-pole-vault maneuver with her umbrella to avoid getting too close. Again, Ada looked like she might call the nuns to arrange an exorcism, because it seemed Molly had been possessed by a malevolent spirit who voluntarily participated in sports.

At lunch, Felicity looked like she might have been crying. Her mascara was smudged, her foundation was patchy, and her eyes were red-rimmed and puffy. Rumor had it she'd been called out of class yesterday afternoon and wasn't seen in school for the rest of the day. Aching with sympathy, Molly wondered if her mom had gotten worse.

Taking a seat next to her rival turned reluctant ally, she lowered her voice and said, "Is everything okay?"

"Why wouldn't it be?" Felicity snapped sharply.

Molly tried not to let the aggression get to her. She remembered riding that roller coaster of emotion all too well. "I'm here to talk if you want."

"When would I ever want that?"

Felicity's tone was so acerbic that it drew Ada's attention to the strangely heated conversation. Molly shot her best friend a look that said everything was fine, but Ada narrowed her eyes, and Molly wasn't entirely sure she bought it.

The telltale dropping of volume signaled the arrival of the Waverleys, who strutted over to the table next to the Populars. The sixth graders who were already sitting there scrambled faster than a pan of eggs, reminding Molly of the weird moment with the displaced mermaids at the clamdunk match the previous night.

"Hey, everyone," said Serena, stifling a yawn. "Hey, Molly."

Both Felicity's and Ada's eyes shot out of their heads at this. Ada kicked Molly's shin under the table as if to say, "Why is Serena Waverley singling you out for special attention? Have I been replaced as best friend? Do I have to shave your head in order to make you a less desirable pal?" Or something.

"Take it you've been to the Seabrooks' fish-and-chip shop, then," Cute Steve said, shoveling a forkful of spicy chicken and rice into his beautiful, beautiful mouth.

"Er, yeah," Finn agreed, shooting Molly a spiky grin. "It was delicious. And we got free chips. Molly's cool."

Felicity scoffed so loudly that a herd of goats in Mumbai probably heard her. "If you call fish tails cool..."

Oh dear.

Please, no, Felicity.

Molly's pulse thumped in her ears. Was she about to be exposed? Just because Finn had inexplicably deemed her cool?

Serena's eyes widened in Molly's direction as if to ask, "Does she know?"

Crossing her fingers under the table, Molly shook her head as subtly as she could. She didn't want them to know that Felicity knew that... Oh no, what a mess.

Fortunately, nobody other than Serena seemed to guess that Felicity meant anything other than Molly's weird job.

Cute Steve shrugged. "I like that she doesn't care about dressing up as a haddock."

Okay. Okay. It's going to be fine.

"Sure," Felicity smirked as she watched Molly squirm. "Just the haddock thing."

Unfortunately, right as Molly shot Felicity a begging look, Ada locked eyes on the pair of them. And in that moment, Molly knew that Ada knew that (*oh wow!*) something was going on. Something bad.

She felt utterly sick at all the clues her best friend could be putting together.

The things she'd overheard. *"What did you just say? Something about mermaids?"*

The things Felicity had said. *"If you call fish tails cool…"*

The things she had witnessed. Molly pole-vaulting over bodies of water, leaping away from the swimming pool, and generally behaving like an absolute lunatic whenever the tide came anywhere near the boardwalk.

It seemed unlikely that Ada would jump to the conclusion that her best friend of so many years was a mermaid. What sane person would possibly think that? Molly herself still wasn't totally convinced that mermaids were real, despite all the evidence to the contrary.

And yet…

There was something in the way Ada was staring at her right now. With such burning curiosity that Molly couldn't help but wonder.

Through the driest mouth of all time, Molly managed to croak out, "Anyway, how did your soccer match go this weekend, Penalty?"

Penalty immediately dropped his fork and yelled at the top of his lungs, "Threeeeee nothing! Threeeeee nothing! Threeeeee nothing!" Not one single person in the surrounding area paid him the slightest bit of attention. Everyone was so used to Penalty randomly turning into a soccer commentator that it wasn't even worth looking up from their mystery spicy chicken.

"You should all come and watch next time," Cute Steve said, gesturing toward Molly, Ada, and the Waverleys, who were whispering between themselves. "Felicity's not inter-ested, are you, babe?"

Good, Molly thought. *What a fantastic thing to say when "babe" is in real danger of outing me as a supernatural freak.*

"Yes, I am," Felicity snarked back indignantly.

Cute Steve stared at her. "This morning, you told me soccer was for the very stupid and the very boring."

Penalty raised an eyebrow. "Boy, that's charming."

"I was joking," Felicity mumbled. "That was about...that referee you guys hate."

"No, it wasn't."

Molly kicked Cute Steve under the table to say, "Please stop antagonizing the person who holds my future in her perfectly manicured hands."

But by then, Felicity had had enough. Practically spitting her words out, she got to her feet and grabbed her Michael Kors tote bag. "Fine. Hang out with that subhuman freak. See if I care." Except there was also another very rude word in there.

Then she stormed out. If this had been a cartoon, there would've been a trail of kicked-up dust in her wake. Jenna and Briony looked at each other, wordlessly deciding whether to follow, but it seemed they were also fed up with Felicity's foul mood, because they stayed put.

Cute Steve pushed his mystery chicken around his tray, pouting slightly. "There's something going on with her," he said. "God knows what. She's been grumpy for weeks now. Crying all the time, won't tell me what's wrong. I can't spend all my time worrying about it."

Jenna and Briony murmured in agreement. Molly thought this was kind of mean of them. She didn't like Felicity all that much, but Steve, Jenna, and Briony were supposed to be Felicity's closest friends. They should have been making sure Felicity was okay and trying to understand why she was so upset and angry all the time rather than complaining behind her back. It's what Ada would—and did—do for her.

Because Molly knew how bad this particular sadness was. She knew how much it sucked to have a mom going through cancer. At least Molly had had the support of her sisters and Ada. She couldn't even imagine coping alone, with not even your boyfriend or best friends knowing enough to support you.

She also knew what it was like to deal with mood swings. To say horrible stuff and immediately regret it, or to not regret it and feel even worse because you're almost definitely broken inside.

Being a teenage girl was hard. Being a teenage girl with a sick mom was even harder. So Molly did the unimaginable. She stuck up for Felicity Davison when nobody else would.

"You should be there for her," she said quietly. "We all go through hard times."

Cute Steve stared at her, as did the rest of the table. "Are you for real?" he said. "She's just been mean to you. That's not right."

Even Jenna and Briony looked astounded. Hopefully they'd report back to Felicity that Molly had her back, and it would make Felicity less likely to expose Molly and/or stab her in the night.

"Well, my sister Margot is awful to me too," Molly said, staring at a very specific rice granule. "But in, like, an affectionate way. I'm used to it. People who are overly nice are weird."

Ada stared at her in astonishment while the Waverleys watched the whole thing unfold, agog, no doubt trying to figure out where Felicity's "subhuman freak" comment fit into everything.

Cute Steve looked at Molly with something resembling admiration. "Yeah, I guess you're right. I'll go see if she's okay."

Then, as he stood up, he added, "You're full of surprises, you know that?"

Molly snorted. "I'm a Seabrook. It comes with the territory."

The Mightiest of Sausages

*A*s the sun had miraculously made an appearance that evening, Molly spent her shift on the Good Ship Haddock. What with the crisp air, twinkling lights, and Eddie of the Ears for company, it was actually not too terrible at all.

The first hour passed in a flash. Eddie was practically the only person in school who didn't seem to want to discuss the Waverleys. Instead, he told stories about how his uncle Ian had bought a cabin up in the country and was running a goat sanctuary from the living room.

However, once the dinner rush was over and the air was distinctly more shivery, Eddie didn't seem to be having quite so much fun. While Molly was used to the monotony and boredom and often used the time to come up with fantastical ghost stories in her head, her copilot was getting restless and fidgety in his trash bag prison.

"You don't have to stick around," Molly said, although she very much wanted him to. "I only have an hour left before I can punch out."

A look of mischief spread across Eddie's face, and his foil fins rustled with excitement. He went up to the railing separating the boardwalk from the beach, leaning over the edge and peering down. "Hey, how many free portions of chips and fried pieces will you give me if I do a trick jump off the railings?"

Molly considered this. "None. Because you'll be dead."

"You could at least have the decency to scatter them into my grave as they bury me," said Eddie. "You know, how some people do rose petals. I would have delicious shards of crispy batter."

"I thought when you died you wanted to be shot out of a cannon into the sea."

"True," Eddie conceded. "The batter might get soggy, then. Seriously, I'm jumping. Haven't you always wanted to see a giant cod dive off a pier?"

"More than I've ever wanted anything in my life."

This seemed to be all the motivation Eddie needed. He clambered extremely inelegantly onto the railings, took a deep breath, then leaped the three yards down to the sand while pulling some kind of skateboarder pose in midair.

"Wheeeeeee—AAAARGHHHHHHHHHHHHH!"

The last syllable was full of anguish. Molly's heart jackhammered into her throat. She sprinted to the railing and followed the noise down. "Eddie?"

In the darkness, she could just make out Eddie of the Ears crumpled in a ball, clutching his calf and whimpering despite clearly trying very hard not to. His foot hung at a strange angle that Margot would probably love to photograph. "My... ankle. Snapped. Owwwwwwwwww!"

Molly was about to dash down the concrete steps to see if he was okay...until she realized how far the tide was coming in. As her legs began to tingle threateningly, she quickly backed away from the sand and on to the boardwalk.

"Just wait there," she called hastily. "I'll call for help!"

"Nooooo, come back!" he yelled. "Come here! Where are you going? Don't leave me here by myself. Help me up."

Molly inched even farther backward. "I—I can't, okay? Just...hold on."

Ignoring his cries, Molly sprinted into the chip shop. The warm air hit her like something physical. It was extremely quiet, so Melissa was cleaning the grill while Margot shoved chips up a giggling Minnie's nose. "Quick," Molly shouted at her sisters. "Eddie's hurt himself."

Weirdly, it was Margot who jumped into action first. She tossed her apron dramatically to the ground, swiveled her cap so it faced backward, and dashed out the door after Molly. Melissa tutted as though the entire debacle was an enormous inconvenience to her.

When Margot saw Eddie buckled over on the sand, she did what Margot always did. Laughed. Hard. "Oh, Edward. How the mightiest of sausages fall."

"We can't go down there," Molly whispered.

Margot's eyes widened. "The tide," she murmured under her breath.

"When you guys are done ogling me..." Eddie grunted.

"Margot," Molly said, louder now so Eddie could hear that she did actually care and wasn't just gathering an audience to witness his misery. "Call an ambulance."

"How?" Margot asked innocently.

"What do you mean, how? Dial nine-one-one."

"And then what?"

Molly couldn't tell whether her sister was messing with her. "For the love of... You'll figure it out."

As Margot went back into the shop to try and locate an ambulance, Minnie came darting out, performing a strange little jig. When she saw Eddie, she cackled hysterically. "Ha-ha-ha. Ankle looks like a donkey."

"Yes," Molly said as patiently as she could. "Exactly. Can you run and get Mom?"

Minnie opened her mouth and bellowed at the top of her lungs. "MOOOOOOOOOMMMMM!"

Even Eddie, in his traumatized state, had to cover his ears with his hands.

Miraculously, Molly's mom appeared at the front door of the lighthouse at the end of the pier. She came shuffling along to where Molly and Minnie stood peering over the railing.

"Oh dear, Edward," Mom said, voice full of maternal concern. "Do you want me to call your mother?"

Eddie winced. "Please don't. Thank you."

"Why not?"

"She told me if I broke any more bones, she'd have me mummified."

"Well, I'll come down there and take a look—"

"Mom," Molly muttered. "The tide. You can't."

Mom clapped a hand to her mouth, shocked at the serious error she'd almost made. "Right you are. I suppose we'll just have to wait up here until the ambulance arrives."

Margot reappeared and told them help was on its way, and Melissa came out to make sure she wasn't missing out on anything juicy. So, the five of them stood in a row, elbows folded over the rail, staring down at the injured boy on the sand below.

Eddie stared at them. "Seriously? Can't any of you come down here and help me up? Or at least bring me a sausage?"

"Er, no," Melissa said nervously. "I think we'll stay up here. But we can drop a sausage down if you like?"

She popped back inside to fetch a battered sausage, then tossed it onto the beach. Considering Melissa was supposed to be a very talented basketball player, Molly was shocked to see the sausage land several feet to Eddie's left, splashing into an overflowing rock pool.

"We're with you in spirit, Edward," Margot added with a grin.

The paramedics finally arrived and lifted Eddie from the beach on a stretcher. He shot Molly a baffled look as he was being piled into the back of the ambulance.

"Your family is strange," he said. Not angry but bemused.

Molly pulled a *yikes* face. "You have no idea."

ℓ·ℓ·ℓ

The next day, Eddie of the Ears made his grand entrance into history on a pair of crutches. He'd taken the morning off from school to pop down to the hospital in the city to have a cast put on his ankle. When he was met by a raucous round of applause, he seemed very pleased with himself and shot Molly an elated grin that said one thing: "Worth it."

As promised, his mother had also mummified his good leg in toilet paper. The woman had a sense of humor. Plus, every time someone walked up the aisle, he "accidentally" moved his plaster-cast clubfoot into their way so they tripped and made an idiot of themselves. Molly, who thought there was nothing funnier than people tripping, found this wildly compelling.

During afternoon recess, Molly and Ada crammed themselves into their locker nook, armed with two bags of salt and vinegar chips and a family-size bag of chocolates. Ada seemed to find the whole "Eddie jumped off the pier for no good reason" thing highly interesting.

"I mean, he was clearly trying to impress you, right?" she said, combining a chip and a chocolate in what was surely a horrifying combination.

"Nah," Molly replied, although she was blushing a little. "It's not like that. He's just a class clown. He would do anything to make anyone laugh."

"Come on," Ada teased, nudging her shoulder. "You're not just anyone. Not to Eddie."

Molly blushed furiously. "What do you mean?"

Ada gave her a knowing look, like their very smug guidance counselor. "You know exactly what I mean."

Green Apple Shampoo

S omehow, the next week went by with almost no drama whatsoever. Ada seemed to forget her bewilderment over Felicity's statements fast enough that she didn't ask any questions, and Felicity herself went from being a vicious shrew to just her regular stone-cold self. Eddie reveled in being the center of attention and bossed Molly around quite a lot, because it was supposedly her fault he was so grievously injured. Every time he waved his crutch at her and demanded a milkshake, Ada shot her a knowing look.

Molly still didn't see the Waverleys all that much in school, since they were older and always surrounded by people. The one or two times they did cross paths, both twins nodded their acknowledgment, but other than the occasional lunchtime appearance, it was all quiet on the Marmouthian front.

For every day that passed without talking to them, Molly grew more and more frustrated. She'd been so close to finding out more about Meire while they were watching clamdunk. But now, it felt like she'd lost her chance.

She needed to focus on plan B: securing an invite to the party of the century. That was the only option. Besides, there were rumors flying around that there would be a bouncy castle, several magicians, and a family of seal pups barking "Silent Night." Who would possibly want to miss that?

Margot had one final clamdunk game before winter vacation next week, and Molly hoped she'd bump into the twins again then. If she did, she would be shameless in hinting about the party, and she'd grab any opportunities for Meire questioning at the same time.

Mom slowly became less and less angry over the trapdoor incident, although she did hold firm on the grounding. Once or twice, Molly asked if she could go and do homework with Ada and Eddie or even if they could come to Kittiwake Keep, since technically, she wouldn't be leaving the house. Mom shot her down at every turn. One night, when Molly came downstairs for a midnight glass of milk, she even found Mom sleeping at the kitchen table, as though guarding the trapdoor.

Thanks to Myla's quick thinking with the rope ladder, the grounding did only last a week, as promised. On her first

Saturday as a free woman, Molly decided to celebrate her release from lighthouse prison by helping Ada's gran deliver Christmas cards for the local church.

It was something of a tradition. Nana Shen was a very short and very kind Chinese lady who was extremely involved in St. Aidan's Church in the center of Little Marmouth. Every year, the elderly folk in the community who couldn't afford stamps could leave their local Christmas cards in a big collection box, and then a group of volunteers would hand deliver them around town. Nana Shen had roped Ada and Molly in when they were seven or eight, and they'd been doing it out of choice ever since.

This year, Ada had invited Eddie to tag along. When his mom dropped him off, Eddie climbed out of the car (with some difficulty) in an old and tattered robin costume he'd found in a local charity shop. His eyes went straight to Molly's with a hopeful upward tilt of his brows, looking for her approval.

"You're not just anyone. Not to Eddie."

Rather than feeling uncomfortable about what Ada had said, the memory spread a burst of warmth through Molly's chest. She'd thought about Ada's words many times. Even though she hadn't known Eddie of the Ears that long, he was already pretty special to her. Everything was just...better when he was around.

But then, the same could be said of Ada. Or Margot. So how could she possibly figure out how she really felt about Eddie? Was it just friendship? Or did the warmth of Ada's words mean it was something more?

The three of them went into the church, which was so cold, Molly half expected to see a frozen woolly mammoth on the altar, and collected a box of cards each. The addresses had been split into streets, and they managed to get three streets in the same part of town so that they could do it together.

It was bitterly cold and sleeting slightly. While Eddie kept warm in his robin suit, Ada and Molly were wrapped up in hats, scarfs, and thick woolen mittens that made it hard to handle the slim envelopes. With Eddie hobbling around on crutches, it was extremely slow going. Still, they got into a good routine, ringing doorbells and sliding cards through letter slots if the recipients weren't home. The windows were full of rainbow-lit Christmas trees, and there were carol singers a few streets over, their voices carrying on the wind.

Seeing how happy Eddie's robin costume made a lot of the older people, Molly began to regret not wearing one herself. She vowed to make or acquire a Rudolph suit for next year.

"Don't you just feel like such a good citizen right now?"

Ada said, rattling her almost-empty box of cards. Her cheeks were like pink apples from the cold, and her hair had flecks of sleet in the tips.

"Absolutely," Eddie said, his breath steaming up in the crisp air around him. "Usually my only contribution to society is keeping certain fish-and-chip shops afloat with my patronage."

Molly grinned. She was carrying both her and Eddie's empty boxes, since he needed both his hands for crutches. "And on behalf of certain fish-and-chip shops, may I say we are eternally grateful."

Eddie sniffed against the cold. "That's the real reason I broke my ankle, you know. I thought it would turn the area into a kind of local landmark. People would come from far and wide to see the spot where famous joker Edward of the Ears almost fell to his death."

"Jumped," Molly corrected. "You mean jumped to his death."

Eddie lifted his chin stoically. There were a few scratches on his jawline from where he'd cut himself trying to shave the three hairs on his chin. "And darn it, Molly, I'd jump again."

Ada watched them knowingly as they bantered back and forth. When Eddie wasn't looking, she flashed a sly wink at Molly. "You two are idiots."

Again, the weird warm glow spread through Molly's chest. She looked up at Eddie, since he was significantly taller than her. There was something about his fluffy bird costume and his scratched jawline and his floppy red hair that just made her feel so...comforted.

He looked down at her right at that precise moment. Their eyes locked in a way they hadn't before. Molly realized she had never really *gazed* until just then. It was a weird feeling. To stare at someone without feeling self-conscious, because they were staring right back at you.

Unfortunately, Eddie's lapse in concentration caused him to land his crutch in the wrong place, and he missed the curb of the sidewalk with his good foot. He collapsed into the road with an *ooft*, and a car had to swerve to avoid running over his head.

Ada didn't know whether to laugh or cry out for help, so she just made a weird strangled noise. Molly leaned down to help Eddie up. As she did, she smelled his green apple shampoo. And, well, the slightly musty scent of a secondhand Christmas costume.

"Do you know, Molly," he said, voice high-pitched with adrenaline, "I'm beginning to think you're not very good for my health."

Their final stop was an address they hadn't visited before.

The house at 9 Second Street was a duplex with a bright-yellow front door and hanging baskets by every window. The rosebushes out front were perfectly trimmed and strung with Christmas lights, and there was a little wooden sign saying "Santa, please stop here!" hanging on the front gate. It was so idyllic, Molly found herself getting a little annoyed.

As they walked/hobbled up the sidewalk, Molly noticed that the yellow paint on the front door was glistening, and someone had taped a sign to the railing saying WET PAINT, PLEASE USE BACK DOOR.

"Oh, for goodness' sake," said Eddie. "Don't they have any respect for the maimed?"

Spotting the narrow sidewalk that wrapped around the house, Molly decided to be a team player. "Don't worry. I'll go," she said. "You guys wait here. Try not to sustain any more injuries."

The backyard was as neat and perfect as the front and backed onto a busy little street dotted with a few shops and cafés. Molly irritably took a sneaky shortcut over a pristine patch of lawn and found herself at a back door—with no mail slot. Sighing, she knocked. She really couldn't be bothered with whatever persnickety middle-aged couple clearly lived here.

But there was another problem.

Molly's legs began to tingle. Hard and fast.

She barely had time to register the fish pond a few yards behind her before she collapsed on the cement with an almighty *ooft*.

Oh dear. Oh no.

If the world was in any way fair, it would've granted Molly a few seconds to dive behind a rosebush before the door above her opened, and the person behind it gasped.

Looking up with dread, Molly gasped too.

It was Finn Waverley.

There was a split second of staring at each other. Molly let out a long breath, realizing this was probably the best-case scenario. Better that another mermaid saw her post-transformation than a pearl-clutching old biddy who'd call the police and/or try to shoo her away with a broom.

"Molly," Finn said, stifling a laugh. "Oh wow, the pond." He took a step back from the doorway, probably to prevent himself from transforming too. "Are your friends still out front?"

"Yeah," Molly grumbled, rubbing the sore spot where her hip had hit the path. "Can you give me a hand, please?"

Finn quickly hoisted Molly inside, shutting the door carefully behind him.

Molly made the snap decision to try and use her merpower again. It hadn't worked at the clamdunk game, but she'd barely known the Waverleys then. Now that she'd spent a little more time with them, it might be easier to read their thoughts.

Hastily, she dug deep in her gut, calling to her merpower to answer her. This time, she tried talking to it. *Please, please let me read his mind. I want to know what he's thinking. I want to see what he knows about Meire and about my family. And to be honest, I want to know whether he thinks I'm a freak.*

The last part sent a flicker of paranoia down her spine. She had no reason to believe Finn thought this, and yet a lifetime of being a part of the strange Seabrook family had left behind some deep-rooted issues.

For a split second, her merpower trembled in response. It wasn't strong—not nearly as breathtaking as the surge at the zoo—but it was *something*.

Unfortunately, her time ran out, and she turned back into an ordinary, powerless teenage girl in the warmth of the Waverleys' very pleasant and homey kitchen.

Close. Closer anyway.

"Are you all right?" Finn asked. "Did anyone see you from the street?"

"I don't think so," Molly muttered, dumping the Christmas card on the kitchen counter. "But I was too busy panicking to look behind me."

"You really have to be more careful," Finn said, though more with concern than anger.

"I mean, you're the mermaids who bought a house with a *pond*," Molly replied irritably. "Seriously. Isn't that impractical?"

Finn laughed. "There aren't many places for sale in Little Marmouth, because nobody ever moves. Come on. You can go out the front. It's lucky your friends didn't come around the back with you."

"Yup," Molly grunted. "So lucky. Struggling to think how I could possibly be luckier."

Sarcasm aside, good luck had definitely been on her side. For nobody to have seen that transformation other than a Waverley twin was nothing short of miraculous.

A Duck in a Blender

That evening, the weather was horrendous, so Molly got to work inside the fish-and-chip shop instead of loitering on the pier and contracting frostbite. The kitchen needed a deep clean, and Molly thought it could be really fun in a weird kind of way. She was, of course, completely mistaken, but it had been a nice thought.

With jingly Christmas songs playing on their beat-up old radio, she was in the process of mopping the grease-coated ceiling when she heard two familiar voices entering the shop.

The Waverleys. Molly's chest skipped with excitement until she realized Melissa was behind the counter. There was no way her sister was going to ignore their mom's advice and be cool about this.

"Hi!" Serena chirped in her overly sweet voice. "Do you do fish-and-chips?"

Melissa's tone was somehow sickly, patronizing, and ice-cold. "First, yes, because we are a fish-and-chip shop. Second, no, we're closed."

"The sign says open," Finn said, more gruff than his sister.

"I forgot to turn it around," Melissa snipped. "I'll do it now."

"I just saw you serve someone two minutes ago," Serena protested, and Molly could almost hear the pout.

Finn added, "There are chips in the fryer."

"For my dinner," Melissa huffed. "I'm very hungry."

As much as Molly didn't really want the Waverleys to see her in the Seabrooks' cap-and-polo-shirt combo, she was going to have to rescue them. She dropped the mop, wiped her brow on her forearm, and headed through to the front. Serena's face lit up at the sight of her.

"Melissa, it's fine," Molly said. "I'll serve them."

Melissa glared viciously, folding her arms across her chest. "But Mom said—"

"They did me and Margot a favor the other night," Molly interrupted before Melissa could say too much about their family's mystery trip with the twins. She shot a look at Finn. "And, erm, again today. Don't worry about it."

Melissa looked like she would very much like to give Molly

a punishment right now. Still, there wasn't much she could do or say to get her sister to back down, so she disappeared through the back with a harrumph. Molly could practically hear her stabbing Mom's name on her phone screen.

"Sorry about that," Molly said, beaming a little too brightly. "She doesn't like newcomers. Or tourists. Sort of a hermit figure, really. She'd be more at home under a bridge, making people answer riddles in order to pass. What can I get for you?"

The twins ordered, and Molly busied herself preparing the food. She scooped the fresh chips out of the fryer, then rolled two big pieces of haddock in flour, dunked them in batter, and dropped them in.

"We had a lot of fun the other night," Serena said. "At the clam—"

"Sausages are niiiiiice! Sausages have...spiiiiiice!" Molly started singing very loudly for fear of Melissa hearing about their illegal clamdunk trip. Why this particular nonsense tune was the first thing to come to mind, she had no idea.

Serena blinked her ultralong lashes. "Are you okay?" she said.

Molly wished she could toss herself in the deep-fat fryer alongside the fish. "I just like to sing."

"Good thing you're so talented at it," Finn said, smirking.

"Thank you," Molly said earnestly, even though she knew

she sounded like a duck caught in a blender when she sang. "I was actually scouted by a major record label last week."

"Wow, really?" Finn asked, eyes widening.

"No," Molly deadpanned. Serena smirked appreciatively. "Want tartar sauce?"

They both nodded, which is how Molly knew they couldn't possibly be as bad as Mom thought.

Serena smiled. "You're funny, Molly. Hey, we're having an end-of-semester party next weekend. Our parents have said it's okay, so don't worry. Your mom should be cool with it!"

Yessssss!

Not even her nonsense singing about sausages had ruined it!

She was in. Officially, truly in…

Still, the thought of showing up alone to a house party full of ninth graders gave her rippling palpitations. So even though it was deeply uncool, she found herself asking, "Can I bring my friends? Ada and Eddie?"

Melissa appeared, scowling, behind the counter.

"Sure!" Serena said enthusiastically, clapping her hands together. Her nails were painted peachy pink. "The more the merrier. M—what did you say your sister's name was?"

"Melissa." Molly finished wrapping up the twins' meals and rang them through the till.

"Melissa? Would you like to come to a special party?" Serena spoke to Melissa like she was a very small hamster who got spooked easily. Molly found this hilarious.

In a startlingly high-pitched voice, Melissa shrieked, "NoandIdon'tthinkanyoneelseshouldeither!"

Serena and Finn exchanged glances.

"I'll be there," Molly said firmly, handing them their warm, newspaper-wrapped packages.

After they left, Melissa detonated. "Molly, what—I mean really, what do you think you're doing? Mom insisted that it wasn't safe to be in contact with the Waverleys, and now not only do I find out that you and Margot have been cavorting—"

"Cavorting," Molly snorted. "Really?"

"I really don't think this is funny, Mollifer!"

Molly gaped at her. "My name is not Mollifer. I was christened Molly. Are you just trying to assert your authority? Or did you...make a joke? It's never happened before, so I'm not sure—"

Against all the odds, the corner of Melissa's mouth quirked. "That depends whether you found it funny or not."

"I find everything you say funny," Molly said honestly.

Melissa looked pleased, not quite realizing that this was not the compliment it seemed to be.

Rebellious Reading

The next day, the world ended.

Not the human world, nor the mermaid one. But Myla's.

Against all the odds and despite straight *A*'s, she didn't get into Cambridge.

This was a tragedy on a par with dinosaur extinction. When Myla opened the letter over her syrupy porridge breakfast, she promptly burst into tears and sprinted upstairs to her room to drown Boudicca in snot. (The rabbit, not the historical figure.) She was so distraught, she wouldn't even let Molly or Mom in.

Molly genuinely felt bad for her sister. Then she spent all day thinking about how school really was pointless. You could work as hard as Myla, dedicating your whole existence to learning, and still not get to where you wanted to be. Molly didn't think anyone in the world, let alone the country, deserved a place at Cambridge more than Myla. She wished there was something she could do to convince them to change their minds or cheer her sister up somehow. But there was nothing.

The whole debacle reminded Molly of the dusty old book Myla had picked out for her before their trip to see Balaena: *The Extremely Unauthorized but Highly Interesting Complete History of Meire*. It was still tucked under Molly's mattress, untouched.

Molly decided that this would be the night she'd finally open it. She was babysitting a sleeping Minnie, Myla was hiding out at the library, Melissa was at a field hockey match that Mom was going to watch, and Margot was running the shop. This was the perfect opportunity to find out more about her homeland while also giving her something to discuss with Myla when she was feeling better.

Once she had made a passing attempt at her homework (i.e., texted Ada and Eddie for the correct answers), Molly ate the leftover chicken potpie Mom had provided for dinner, made a cup of milky tea, checked quickly on Minnie, then headed up to her room to voluntarily read a book for probably the first time in her life.

It was warmer in the living room by the woodstove, but Molly wanted the chance to hide the book when she heard her mom and sisters come back in. Since her mom had installed the alarm on the trapdoor, she didn't want to answer any questions about how she'd gotten her hands on the book to begin with.

Rebellious reading. Who had she become?

She made a blanket nest using both her and Melissa's duvets and propped up a bunch of pillows behind her head. Carefully, she pulled the old book out of its hiding place beneath her mattress. She ran a finger over the gold foil title, shivering with anticipation. It was bound in cracked midnight-blue leather and studded with fragments of pearly shells.

However, when she opened it, she found it impossible to read. It was in a different language entirely. Flicking dejectedly through the first few chapters, Molly's heart sank. It suddenly made sense that Myla used her merpower—understanding every mythical sea language—to read it.

Her sister had made some annotated translations in the margins, so Molly tried her best to piece those together. From what she could gather, a great ruler named Aquata had brought together several smaller mermaid nations in the North Sea and formed a mighty empire named Meire. There were inky black maps on old sepia paper, with place names like Tempaesta, Naevis, Delphaena, and Chimaera.

Despite the annotations, it was slow going. Molly was about to close the book when she flipped to an interesting page. It looked like a family tree.

The thing that caught her eye the most was a familiar word: *Marefluma*. It was used as a surname for the past six empresses: Mira Marefluma, Marilla Marefluma, Myra Marefluma, Morwenna Marefluma, and Mericia Marefluma.

Where had Molly heard or read that word before? It could just have been from scanning the book tonight, but she was sure it had lodged in her brain well before that. It had such an oceanic, lyrical sound, unlike any English word she'd heard.

Try as she might, she couldn't recall where she might have stumbled upon it. Eventually, she gave up, stashed the book back under her mattress, and ran herself a bath, nice and deep so that she would transform. For some reason, she thought that spending time as a mermaid might trigger her memory of the word *Marefluma*, but it was no use. She simply couldn't put her fin on it.

A Snoring Manatee

*M*arefluma. Where had she seen that word before?

Molly tried texting and calling Myla, but her sister's phone was switched off. She wished there was a mermaid Google, because when she ran a search for "Meire and Marefluma" on regular Google, it told her the phrase did not match any documents. This was surely the first time that had ever happened to anyone. Even keyboard mashing usually brought up some interesting reads. (That was how she'd discovered how snails reproduce.)

Molly knew she'd never be able to sleep tonight without answers, so she decided to wait up for Myla to come home. Unfortunately, that didn't happen. Molly resigned herself to a sleepless night.

Melissa and Mom arrived home from Melissa's field

hockey match at nearly midnight, absolutely soaking wet and in furious moods. They slammed into the kitchen, dripping everywhere. Mom put the kettle on with so much aggression, it was as though the appliance had personally wronged her. Melissa wore a sling on her right arm, and her eyes were red-raw from crying.

Molly pieced together various sound bites. Not only had SPLuM lost spectacularly, but the waterlogged pitch had caused Melissa to transform into a mermaid. She had managed to logroll into a large pile of gym bags before anyone could see what had happened, but it had still been an absolute nightmare, trying to insist she was fine and just having a little rest.

When everyone had given up, Mom then had to haul her by the arms toward the building until she switched back to human mode. In the process, she had dislocated Melissa's shoulder. They had then spent two hours in the emergency room, waiting to have it popped back into place. Judging by the haunted look on Melissa's face, this was much more painful than the word *pop* suggested.

All in all, a great evening.

Molly gave up on Myla and went to bed. As predicted, she got no sleep whatsoever. Not just because the Marefluma question was burning in her mind but because the painkillers had transformed Melissa into a snoring manatee.

The next morning, Molly tracked Myla down in the senior year homeroom. Usually seventh graders weren't allowed in, but she hung around the door until another senior appeared, then said there was a family emergency and she needed to speak to her sister. The student—a burly soccer player with a broken nose and squashed cauliflower ears—didn't seem to care about the ageist rules and led Molly straight in.

The room was a big square, with two walls made up of cubbyholes for students to stash their books in, the third wall lined with workstations, and the fourth with a small kitchenette for making cups of coffee and tea. There were haggard, torn blue sofas from IKEA, plus a bunch of bulletin boards full of exam schedules, sports rosters, and other twelfth-grade-only announcements, like how cooking shin guards in the communal toaster was banned until further notice.

Myla was tucked away in the far corner of the common room, where the workstations met the cubbyholes, furiously scribbling an essay. Her glasses had slipped down to the tip of her nose, and her hair was a frizzy mess in a corkscrew bun. If this was a cartoon, Molly would probably have been able to see the bluebottle flies circling her head. She most definitely had not showered in days.

Molly approached cautiously, as though her sweet sister was instead a rabid wolf. A rabid wolf that had not showered in days.

"Myla?" Molly whispered, pulling out the chair next to her.

Myla leaped up as though waking from a deep sleep. "Molly? What are you—is everything okay? Oh no, is it Mom?"

Ever since Mom's cancer diagnosis, they'd all been a little jumpy every time bad news was announced or someone turned up unexpectedly, or even if a sister had an unreadable expression on her face.

"No," Molly said, eager to put Myla's mind at ease. "I lied about a family emergency to get in here, but there's nothing actually wrong."

Myla slumped. "So why?" she asked, like her energy had been sapped by a river leech.

"I have something I need to talk to you about," Molly whispered. She was unable to stop the excited look from spreading across her face. "I read the book."

"I'm so proud of you," Myla gushed. "It's not an easy read."

"Well, by read, I mean skimmed your notes in the margins. Not everyone has your merpower. But there was one word I recognized on a family tree, and I can't remember where from. It's probably nothing, but…"

"What's the word?"

"Marefluma?" Molly tried, stumbling over the pronunciation.

Myla frowned. "Like on my telescope?"

Of course! It was engraved on Myla's peculiar telescope, the one she got from Murielle.

"What does it mean?" Molly asked.

Myla's brain was ticking louder than a grandfather clock. "I'm not sure. Leave the book in my room later, and I'll have another look."

"It must be something, right?" Molly chattered excitedly. "If you got the telescope from Murielle."

Myla smiled, but it was tight and forced. "Yeah. Maybe."

Molly softened her voice as much as she could to ask, "How are you doing?"

Myla bit her top lip, staring down at the essay she'd been so maniacally tearing through. "I'm sad. Really sad."

"Would a trip to see Balaena cheer you up?"

"I don't know, Mol." Myla sounded defeated and small. "If I want the best chance possible of making it into my second-choice college, I need to be studying. Clearly, I've been taking too much time off as it is. I'm so angry at myself."

"Don't be ridiculous!" Molly insisted. "You work harder than anyone else I know. You're going to be fine, Myla. Better than fine. You're going to get another offer, I know it. Even if it's not from Cambridge."

"Thanks, Mol. Sorry not to be more excited about the Marefluma thing. I'm sure we'll get to the bottom of it."

Even though Molly wanted so badly to see Balaena again and to ask Myla a million more questions about Meire, she knew she had to respect her sister's wishes. She squeezed Myla's hand. It was cold and shaky. "I understand."

A Dangerous Thing to Discuss

*K*nowing that she'd secured an invite to the most exclusive party in SPLuM's history did something funny to Molly. She held her head higher as she walked through the hallways, feeling smug as she listened to the panicked conversations of those who'd been snubbed.

Ada noticed her improved posture and asked if she'd been taking tips from the Instagram influencer who said you should stuff slices of bread in the heels of your shoes so you walked taller. Molly loved being able to tell her that no, it was because she'd *somehow* gotten them invited to the end-of-semester party at 9 Second Street. Ada squealed like a banshee at the news and immediately began to plan potential outfits.

At lunch, Molly ate with Ada and the Populars, who now took over two big cafeteria tables to accommodate the

Waverleys and their entourage. Cute Steve and Penalty Pete were embroiled in a heated conversation about some kind of soccer match, and Felicity, Jenna, and Briony were in low talks about something inaudible. Molly really hoped it was about Felicity's mom. She deserved to have friends she could talk to about what she was going through.

Finn and Serena were airily discussing how they were settling into Little Marmouth, and their entourage was lapping it up. Their fans included Cauliflower Ears, who was staring lovingly at Finn as though a rainbow shone from his mouth, and a few other twelfth graders. Finn was talking about their old school. "We miss our old friends, obviously. We're hoping the party will help us make new ones."

"What about your boyfriend?" asked Cauliflower Ears in a gruff, brazen way, and Finn smirked playfully at him. "Will he be at the party too?"

"And we miss our grandparents," Serena added. "They live farther down the coast. We miss them a lot. Especially Nana's sea-salt fudge."

"My dad makes fudge," said a sparkly legged senior Molly didn't recognize. "I'll bring you some."

Serena didn't even notice that Sparkles had spoken. Instead, she turned to Molly, a weird expression on her pretty Viking features. "Do you ever miss Murielle, Molly?"

Molly froze, a forkful of chili con carne halfway to her mouth.

How did Serena know Murielle's name? Molly herself had never heard it until a few weeks ago. She racked her brains. Had she used the name when they were at the clamdunk match?

In any case, it was a dangerous thing to discuss at school, and Molly did not recover very quickly. "I...erm?"

"That is your grandmother's name, isn't it?" Serena asked innocently.

Molly swallowed. Ada was looking at her weirdly, having no doubt never heard Molly talk about her grandmother. "I think...yes, yes it is. I didn't hear you correctly. I actually haven't seen her in years." *Well, ever.*

Serena gave a conspiratorial smile. "You should really make the effort to visit."

Molly felt a spike of fear. There was something about the sickly-sweet expression on Serena's face, the slightly smug look on Finn's... Was she walking into a trap?

She couldn't be. The Waverleys couldn't out the Seabrooks without outing themselves too. They were just being playful, poking fun at the ignorant humans' expense. Talking in subtext and secrets just because they could.

Even when the conversation moved on, the hot, prickly

feeling stayed with Molly. Sooner or later, Ada was going to start piecing all these shards of information together. Even if she didn't guess exactly what was going on, she would surely know that Molly was hiding something from her. Something big.

She couldn't fight the feeling that this was all about to blow up in her face.

And soon.

The Elderly Residents of Beirut

On yet another cold and soggy evening, Margot and Molly were holding down the chip-shop fort alone. Molly was still painstakingly deep cleaning the entire building, which, while disgusting and greasy and heavy on the bluebottle flies, was still better than losing a finger to frostbite.

Well, mostly. There had been the decades-old burger bun she found behind a counter, which looked like something aliens might use as a biological weapon. Molly thought she'd happily lose a pinky never to have to touch that thing again.

Between customers, Margot came through the back to "help" Molly, which largely involved eating chips and pointing out how bad her sister was at cleaning. To be fair, Molly was barely listening. She was on the cusp of piecing together why Mom was so fearful of the Waverleys and of her daughters going in the sea. And she couldn't help feeling that Murielle was at the heart of it.

It was Murielle's telescope that bore the word *Marefluma* and her name that the Waverleys had so flippantly used at lunch. And hadn't Myla said there had been some kind of fight between Mom and Murielle? Something that made them leave Meire?

Yet Myla still hadn't reread the book, so Molly was no further forward in solving the mystery once and for all. Maybe if she could see Balaena one more time…

"Don't suppose you feel like sneaking out again tonight?" Molly said to Margot, vaguely aware that she'd interrupted her sister midsentence. "I have a hankering to use the rope ladder."

Margot stared at her. "May I remind you that you screamed silently the whole way down last time?"

"With exhilaration," Molly lied. "Sure."

"Please?"

Margot stared intently at the bag of chips in her hand. They were absolutely drenched in salt and vinegar, and she chewed them very slowly. "Why?"

Molly thought she heard a trace of suspicion in Margot's voice. "I want to show you something."

"Where?"

It was interesting that she used the word *where* instead of *what*. Molly remembered how Margot had admitted the deep sea scared her. It was weird and new, thinking of her no-nonsense sister as someone who had fears.

"Just a little bit farther out to sea," Molly said in a bid to calm Margot's nerves. "You'll love it, Margs, I swear."

Margot squared her shoulders as if to remind Molly who was boss. "I've told you. I don't like going out to the dangerous parts."

"Not even for a glimpse of your homeland?" Molly said eagerly.

This had the exact opposite effect to the one she intended. Margot immediately froze. "So that's what this is about."

"What?"

"Your obsession with Meire."

"I'm not obsessed!"

"Molly, you read a book. An actual piece of literature."

Now it was Molly's turn to harrumph. "How do you know that?"

"Please," Margot said, rolling her eyes for the hundredth time in the conversation. "It's as if you think I don't search your room every night for new ways to booby-trap it."

"So what if I'm interested in where we came from?" Molly argued, on the defensive now.

"It's not just *interest*!" Margot snapped. "Sneaking out with Myla, practically stalking the Waverleys... It's like nothing else matters to you anymore."

"Margot, come on—"

"Why isn't our life on land enough?" Margot asked, and Molly swore her voice cracked just a little.

"It is!" Molly insisted. "It's just—"

"I don't care. I don't." Margot finished off her vinegary chips and hopped off the counter. "I'm grateful for the life we have now. The six of us, in the Keep. And I don't see the need to put myself in danger just for a tiny glimpse of what might have been."

Molly smirked. This was a whole new side to Margot. Who knew she had actual literal emotions? "That was very poetic and meaningful."

"Whatever," Margot muttered, not rising to the bait. "Do what you want. Just don't come crying to me when it all goes wrong."

Molly spent the rest of the night in an awful mood. She hated fighting with Margot. Still, there were only a few days of school left before vacation, and she had the Waverleys' party to look forward to on the weekend. Ada was still extremely excited, unlike Eddie, who didn't understand the fascination with the twins. But he was happy that Molly and

Ada were happy and started trolling them with an impressive variety of terrible outfit ideas. So far, Molly had vetoed a trilby hat belonging to his grandfather, a full wet suit and flippers, and Joseph's Amazing Technicolor Dreamcoat from a youth theater production he'd starred in the previous winter.

Of course, Felicity would be there too. For a while, Molly was a little concerned that she wouldn't survive an entire evening without Felicity exposing her to the world. After all, in their last interaction, Felicity had loudly called Molly a subhuman freak in front of everyone. So, it was fair to say their peace treaty was on rocky ground.

However, one morning before first bell, Felicity approached Molly at the sink in the girls' bathroom.

"Hey," Molly said uncertainly. She really wanted to ask how Felicity's mom was but thought it was maybe best not to. They were the only two people in the bathroom. If Felicity wanted to kick her head in, now was an excellent time.

"Hi," Felicity said.

Molly couldn't read her tone. "I...erm...what's up?"

Felicity checked her reflection in the mirror. Then she started to wash her hands, even though she hadn't peed. She seemed almost nervous. Eventually, she cleared her throat and said, "Jenna and Briony told me what you did. Standing up for me with Steve. Getting him to come after me. You didn't have to do that."

"Oh," said Molly, very eloquently and insightfully. "Well, I wanted to."

"Why?"

Molly searched for the right words. "I just...remember. How sad it makes you. And you should have people around you who support you, no matter what."

"Yeah," Felicity muttered, applying yet more soap to her cuticles. "I think I'm going to tell them."

"That's good," Molly said. "You should. It helps."

Of course, the unspoken words rattling around Molly's head were *If word gets out about her mom, then she has no reason to keep my tail a secret. Oh no!* But she didn't want to ruin the rare nice moment with her world-ending concerns, so she kept quiet.

"You're a good person," Felicity mumbled, as though she didn't really want Molly to hear. For a split second, she looked like she might hug Molly or at least apologize for calling her a subhuman freak. But in the end, she thought better of it and fled the emotional conversation with her hands still dripping wet.

Molly relaxed. Maybe their truce wasn't in trouble, after all.

Still, there was one person who Molly worried *would* find

out her secret. A person she had fought for so long to hide it from and who was surely on the brink of figuring it out.

ele

"How come Serena knows your grandma?" Ada asked, crunching through a pack of crackers when the two of them were tucked into their locker nook at morning break. "You've never mentioned her before."

"Yeah," Molly said vaguely. "It's my mom's mom. We never see her."

"Why not?"

"She lives too far away." This was, at the very least, not a lie.

"Where?"

After too long a pause in which Molly could not think of a single other place besides Little Marmouth, she eventually said, "Lebanon." She'd meant to say London, but it came out a little bit wrong, so she just had to roll with it.

"Wow," Ada said, visibly impressed to the point where she sprayed cheese puff all over Molly's face. "So how does Serena know her?"

Really, Molly? Lebanon? How could she possibly explain how the Waverleys were familiar with the elderly residents of Beirut? "I think our grandparents went to school together or something," she said noncommittally.

"Hmm."

Molly was sure she overheard words like *mermaid* and *subhuman freak* whirring around in her best friend's memory. In a strange way, she felt almost jealous of Felicity. Her secret was hers to tell, and she could confide in her best friends if and when she wanted to. But Molly...Molly still had to hide this huge part of herself from the person she cared for the most.

She crossed everything that both Felicity and Serena would stay true to their words and keep quiet on the weekend. The last thing she needed was for Ada to have one more piece of the puzzle ready to put into place.

CHAPTER

20

We're So Cool and Mature

The last day of school involved watching movies in class, an extremely long choir concert, and a becrutched Eddie of the Ears being sent home for dressing as a robin. This made Molly laugh a lot.

Walking out of the school gates toward two and a half weeks of freedom was a high unlike any other. Molly practically skipped home to Kittiwake Keep, a disgruntled Margot by her side. Things hadn't been the same since their disagreement about Balaena, but Molly wasn't about to let that get to her. It was Christmas, she was free, and she had her first real house party to go to. Life was good.

Saturday morning absolutely dragged. Molly did a shift on the Good Ship Haddock, but Ada and Eddie didn't visit like they usually did, since they were all seeing each other later. Even the ice cream kiosk was closed—something to do with a flooded blending machine—so there was no Cute Steve to ogle. The handful of walkers who strayed from the busy main street shot her a lot of sympathetic looks, and she imagined she looked pathetic with raindrops dripping from the end of her nose, a soggy wedge of leaflets clutched in her shivering fin.

In the afternoon, she took a hot shower to thaw out and headed over to Ada's to get ready—and borrow something to wear. Molly's closet consisted mainly of faded T-shirts and hand-me-down jeans from Margot, who had much smaller hips than Molly did, so Molly often had to keep the button closed with a stretchy hair tie. It was a very strong look. Extremely regal.

Molly, for one, was very grateful for school uniforms, because if they wore their own clothes, she would be even more shunned than she was right now.

Molly told Mom she was staying at Ada's tonight, which was technically true. It was just that there would be a short excursion in between, to a house party at the residence of Mom's sworn enemies. She really struggled to feel guilty about this lie by omission. Mom still refused to tell her why the sea was a dangerous hellhole and the Waverleys were Satan incarnate. If grown-ups couldn't be honest, why should teenagers?

Bundled up in her biggest puffy coat, Molly trekked

through town to Ada's house with her overnight duffel bag slung over her shoulder.

"You're here!" Ada greeted her at the door—a big faux Tudor thing—still in her pajamas, bouncing around like Tigger. "Ohmygosh, I'm so excited. Can you believe it? We're going to an actual house party. And not, like, my little cousin's birthday party. An actual house party."

Molly closed the door behind her and shrugged her coat onto the coatrack. The house was warm and smelled like homemade tomato soup. Ada's dad was always cooking. "And are you okay? You seem a little…frantic."

"Coffee!" Ada exclaimed, eyes wide and almost entirely pupil. "I drink coffee now. It's part of my new persona as a person who attends house parties. Would you like a cup?"

"Sure," Molly agreed. She had never had coffee, because her mom said it was too strong and much more addictive than tea, but this was a day for defying her mother. Why not start now?

"Great!" Ada did a little leap of excitement before skidding through into the empty kitchen. The counter was in disarray from the soup preparation and also from Ada's attempt at using the cappuccino maker. "Coffee is so great. You'll see. And if you put enough gingerbread syrup in it, you can't even taste the coffee at all."

"Perfect," Molly said. "We are so cool and mature."

"I was just thinking that. Next, we'll be having wine and cheese parties. I do like a good Brie."

A bubble of nerves popped in Molly's stomach. There was something she had been worried about, something she wasn't sure she was willing to defy her mom on just yet. "Do you think there will be wine tonight?" she said.

"Keep your voice down, will you?" Ada hissed. "My dad will ban us from going if he thinks there'll be alcohol."

Molly hopped up onto the big quartz-topped island. It was covered in flour from Mr. Shen's homemade sourdough, and a puff of white cloud rose around her. "Will you drink any if there is some?"

Ada chewed the inside of her cheek as she poured milk into the frother. "I don't know. I've only had it twice before."

"Twice!" gasped Molly. "And you didn't tell me! Anything else I should know about? Have you smoked a cigarette? Gotten your foot pierced?"

Ada popped a big clay mug under the cappuccino machine. It started whirring and gushing. "It wasn't that big a deal. It was at my uncle's fiftieth. He got really drunk and gave me a vodka and Coke."

Molly's eyes widened. "What was it like?"

"Imagine mixing a perfectly good Coke with paint stripper. That's what it was like."

Molly laughed as she watched Ada pour an ungodly amount of syrup in her coffee. "But did it make you feel any different?"

"Not really. But I only had a sip, then poured it in a plant pot. The cactus died soon after that, so I probably did the right thing." She handed Molly the coffee/sugar juice. "Coffee is way better. Trust me."

"Anyway," Molly said, taking the mug. "The twins said their parents would be around, so we're probably safe on the paint-stripper front."

"Phew. The cacti of Little Marmouth can breathe easy."

After they'd finished the coffee, which was so sweet it made Molly's teeth cry, they padded upstairs to get ready. Eddie was arriving in an hour, and Molly wanted to be in full party attire by then so that he would think she just naturally looked great (even though, having seen her in the haddock suit umpteen times, he knew this to be untrue). Again, Molly wondered why she cared what Eddie thought. Shouldn't she be obsessing over what look Cute Steve would like most?

Ada laid out a selection of clothes for Molly to choose from. There was an upsetting quantity of tracksuits, which Molly knew with all certainty she was not edgy enough to pull off, and a lot of floral items, which Molly knew with even more certainty she was not girly enough to pull off. She was about to give up when she found a pair of high-waisted jeans and a cropped white mohair sweater that she liked. Fashion expert Ada finished off the look with an oxblood belt, a jumble of necklaces, and some black leather ankle boots, which were a little too tight but looked killer.

They decided to leave Molly's wild curls as they were, because Ada insisted that the style was all the rage at the moment. Ada also floofed up Molly's already-bushy eyebrows with some kind of clear gel and combined that with some mascara and a lick of rose-colored lipstick.

Ada chose some vintage-looking jeans and a mustard-yellow-and-white striped T-shirt. She finished the look by straightening her long, glossy black hair and applying vivid purple lipstick—"My dad is too scared to tell me to take it off for fear of being called sexist." They then proceeded to take a million selfies, which Molly forbade Ada from posting on the off chance her mom saw and figured out their game.

Eddie arrived. True to form, Ada's dad let him come straight up to the bedroom for fear of insinuating that a male friend was any different from a female friend. Ada had him wrapped around her little finger. Molly applauded Ada's tactics, trying to imagine a world in which her mother was not a tyrant and a dictator.

Eddie's eyes widened when he walked in and saw Molly

chilling at the dressing table, all cool lipstick and big brows. "Hey, Mol. You look…" He then seemed to remember Ada was a person who existed. "Wow, you both look nice. With the clothes. And the hair."

"My hair is the same as always." Molly grinned, that weird, warm feeling spreading through her chest and into her stomach.

"I know." Eddie grinned back, rubbing the back of his head bashfully. "That's why it's nice."

Ada laughed and rolled her eyes. "What a sap."

"Shut up," Eddie mumbled, dropping his crutches and taking a perch on the bed. He then seemed to think this was too intimate and slid down to the floor in one fluid motion. If this hurt his broken ankle at all, he didn't show it.

"Do you want a cup of coffee?" Ada asked chirpily.

Molly frantically shook her head behind Ada's back. If Eddie valued his teeth and/or tongue in any way, he should almost definitely say no.

Heeding Molly's warning with a smile, Eddie politely said, "No thank you, dear."

Lavender Bubble Bath

The three of them rang the Waverleys' doorbell. Molly swung her head up and down the street (not literally) to make sure her mom hadn't somehow followed them here.

Someone answered the yellow door. And it was not who Molly expected. Not at all.

"Hello, kids! I'm Mr. Waverley. Serena and Finn will be so happy you made it!"

It was the deliveryman. The deliveryman who'd knocked on the kitchen window all those weeks ago, back when they were all accidentally transformed into mermaids. He, too, had icy eyes, sharp teeth, and chiseled features. And he was grinning straight at her in a knowing kind of way.

Molly didn't understand what this meant. All she knew was that it made her feel extremely uneasy.

Mr. Waverley led them through to a big living room that seemed to be like a den for the kids. Penalty Pete, Felicity, Jenna, and Briony were already there, with Felicity sitting in a round swivel chair directly on top of Cute Steve. There was also a bunch of seniors, including Cauliflower Ears, who was staring misty-eyed at Finn. Everyone was perched on sofa arms and curled cross-legged on the floor, looking much more at home than Molly felt.

A soccer match was playing on TV, so Penalty Pete did not even notice Ada's entrance. There was a huge ice bucket filled with cans of sparkling juice in the corner—none of the alcoholic variety, Molly was relieved to see—so the three of them grabbed some sodas and found an inconspicuous spot by some beanbags in the bay window overlooking the street. Everyone else was just sort of chatting and laughing among themselves, and with the exception of Felicity shooting dirty looks at Molly's newfangled eyebrows, nobody paid them the slightest bit of attention.

Soccer and soda. Molly didn't know what she thought a house party would be like, but it was not this. Maybe she'd been picturing the red plastic cups, Ping-Pong tables, and loud music from TV shows. In any case, she felt a little disappointed and also a little silly for dressing up. Everyone else was in jeans or sweats. She couldn't help thinking the best part of the day was over: getting ready with her friends, drinking sugary coffee, and laughing over Eddie of the Ears' awkwardness.

She also couldn't shake the discombobulating feeling that Mr. Waverley had given her. Everywhere she looked, she saw reminders of who she really was. The room was nautical-themed, with bowls full of white seashells and silver anchor ornaments on the windowsill. There was a painting of a mermaid hanging over the swivel chair. The mermaid was wearing a crown, with dozens of loyal mermen standing guard around her.

Eddie watched her closely, as if sensing Molly's discomfort. It only heightened her anxiety. Her chest felt tight, and her stomach felt like it was gripped in a vise. She was clammy and prickly.

"You okay?" Eddie asked quietly. He looked like he might be about to reach out and squeeze her hand. Molly actually thought that would be quite nice.

"Yeah. Yeah, sorry. Just a little too warm, I think. Do you know where the bathroom is?"

Serena, who obviously had bat-like hearing, called over from the sofa, "It's straight upstairs. The lock's broken, though, so nobody go in after her or you'll get a live show!"

Everyone laughed, even though Molly didn't think it was

very funny. She tucked her chin to her chest and pressed her way across the room, fidgeting awkwardly with the oxblood belt that now felt much too tight.

Once she was out of the living room, she could breathe a little easier. She padded up the bare wooden staircase, steadying her rapid-fire heartbeat. Practically sprinting up the last few steps, Molly dashed into the old-fashioned bathroom and pressed the door shut behind her.

That was odd. The lock looked like it had been intentionally damaged, with one half of the sliding mechanism unscrewed and sitting innocently on the edge of the sink.

And there was something else...

The smell of lavender bubble bath. And the strong, inescapable tingling in her legs.

Too late, Molly turned around and saw an enormous rolltop bath, larger than any she'd ever seen, full to the brim with steaming water.

Before she could stagger back to the landing, she transformed, white glittery mermaid tail flopping into life. She let out a small cry and fell to the ground.

She knew then. She knew with heartrending certainty that this was no accident.

It was a trap. It was a trap. It was a trap, and she had walked right into it.

The Waverleys were trouble. She should've listened.

Footsteps pounded on the stairs, confirming Molly's worst fears.

They were trying to expose her. Actively trying to show the world she was a mermaid. The references to Murielle had been a warning she had not heeded.

But why? Why would they do that?

She only understood one thing. The Waverleys were trying to get the Seabrooks banished back to Meire. And as someone climbed the final step onto the landing, Molly knew it was about to work.

It's Complicated

As she tried desperately to find a towel to cover herself with—they had all been removed—Molly's throat closed up. She whimpered, trying and failing to stop the tears from falling.

She was such an idiot. She'd done this to herself. She'd done this by not listening to her family, by following her own selfish instincts instead of thinking through the worst-case scenario. Because this? This was the worst-case scenario.

The door swung open. In that moment, it felt like the whole world stopped. Molly didn't even dare to look up at whoever was standing there. Felicity, Serena, and Finn already knew, so it was guaranteed to be someone else.

"Molly?" came an awed whisper.

Ada.

Relief crested in Molly's chest.

Her best friend. This was the best-case scenario within the worst-case scenario.

She'd always wanted to tell Ada but had never been able to. Maybe this was a blessing.

"Ada..." Molly whispered.

Ada's voice was rigid with shock. The door hung wide open. "Serena said she thought she heard you crying..."

"I—"

"Wh-what's going on?"

Molly wrapped her arms around herself and shuffled away from the open door's line of sight. "Can you close the door, please?"

In a robotic trance, Ada closed the door, then slumped onto the toilet seat. "Molly..."

"I know," Molly said, unsure where to even begin. She remembered the feeling of deep shock all too well. "I know this looks insane. It *is* insane."

Ada shook her head, her poker-straight locks swishing under the light. "You're... This is a prank. Margot put you up to this?"

When she had first seen her sisters and mother transform, that had been Molly's first thought too. "No. It's real.

I'm a mermaid. I transformed because of the bathtub. It happens whenever we're near a big body of water."

"That's not...no."

Molly started talking very fast, trying to get all the information out at once but not really knowing what to include. "I found out on my birthday. We're all mermaids. My family, I mean. Mom is a mermaid, my dad isn't. Which makes me half."

"Mermaids aren't real." Ada's voice was fierce, as though she was trying to convince herself.

Molly laughed weakly to lighten the mood. "I know."

"But I'm seeing it," Ada murmured, staring at Molly's tail so intensely, it made Molly squirm. "With my own two eyes."

"You can touch it," Molly offered self-consciously, even though the thought was weirdly intimate and made her a little uncomfortable.

"Your birthday was months ago," Ada said in a hurt voice. "You didn't tell me."

"I'm not supposed to tell anyone. It's complicated."

"But this is me we're talking about!"

"I know. I'll explain everything, Ada, I promise." Molly was trying to stay patient and understanding, but she remained painfully aware that with every passing moment, there was a greater chance of another person coming upstairs. It wouldn't be Finn or Serena, because then they'd transform, too, but they would send someone else soon. They would want as many people as possible to bear witness to this.

Wait.

The "wet paint" sign on the front door, back when she was delivering Christmas cards. The pond. The Waverleys had tried this before; it just hadn't worked.

She needed to make sure it didn't work this time, either.

"Right now, I'm in trouble," she said hurriedly. "The government lets us live on land as long as we keep our identities a secret. If we're discovered, we get banished back to Meire, the mermaid queendom in the sea. And it's really, really dangerous now, because of all the pollution. We can't get banished. We can't. Our life on land—it's too special."

As she said the words, she suddenly understood why Margot had been so upset with her. Now that everything was at risk, the thought of losing what they had was agonizing.

Ada seemed to snap back to her usual pragmatic self at this. "Okay, okay. What do you need me to do?"

"I need you to unplug the bathtub, then sit behind the door to make sure nobody else comes in. Once the water's gone, I'll transform back."

"Okay. I can do that." Ada crossed the room, rolled up her sleeve, and fished around in the bottom of the lavender-scented water until she found the plug. She pulled it out with a satisfying plop. "Wow, how unlucky that there was a full tub of water."

Molly grimaced. "Not unlucky. This was a trap. Finn and Serena, they're mermaids, too. For some reason, they want to expose the Seabrooks and have us banished. Mom has been warning me for weeks to stay away from them, but I didn't listen."

"Standard Molly." Ada sighed. "But wait, the Waverleys... Is *everyone* a secret mermaid?"

"No, just us and them." *And Amy Fairbairn*, Molly thought, but that wasn't her secret to tell.

Beneath the blatant shock, Ada still looked betrayed. She'd really taken it to heart—not knowing this major thing about her best friend in the world. Not being trusted with the truth. After her parents had kept their divorce a secret from her for so long, Molly knew this would be a real trigger for Ada.

"I'm sorry," Molly mumbled. "I'm really, really sorry."

"I understand why you couldn't tell me." Ada sniffed, and Molly noticed she was a little teary. "I just wish you'd trusted me, you know? I wouldn't have told anyone. I still won't."

Molly softened her voice. "I know you would never, at least on purpose. But it's such a huge thing to try and keep quiet. I slip up all the time. It's only natural to make mistakes." A loaded pause. "Plus, we had that big fight."

Right after Molly found out she was a mermaid, she and Ada had a huge blowup and didn't speak for weeks. They'd both been at fault, with each of them saying something horrible and regretting it.

Ada cringed. "Oh my gosh. That was after you just found out?"

"Yeah. And then when we made up, I didn't want to risk ruining it."

"Molly. I'm sorry," said Ada. "I should've been there for you. I should've known something serious was up."

Molly smiled despite the sad feeling. "How could you ever guess this?"

There were more footsteps on the stairs. Molly's heart spiked with fear. Serena had sent more people up to witness Molly's humiliation. Maybe some of them even had their phones out, ready to film her.

Oh no, oh no, oh no...

The tub was taking forever to drain, and her tail showed no sign of disappearing yet. The constant adrenaline surges and drops were exhausting and making her ridiculously emotional. The mere sound of someone—no, *multiple* someones—approaching made Molly burst into fresh tears.

"Don't worry," Ada said soothingly. "Nobody is coming in until it's safe."

There was a soft tap at the door, and a voice asked, "Are you guys okay?"

Felicity.

And then, right behind her, Jenna and Briony, gossiping about which of them Finn liked more.

"Mol's just not feeling well," Ada called. "Give us a minute, yeah?"

"No worries," Felicity called back, and for a moment, Molly thought the crisis was averted.

Until she heard Serena's voice on the stairs.

"Honestly, guys, just go in," she said, so sickly sweet that Molly had no idea why she hadn't seen right through it before. "Maybe you can help Molly?"

"No, it's fine," called Ada through gritted teeth. "Please, leave us alone."

"Are you sure everything's all right up there?" Serena cooed. "You sound *super* concerned. Felicity, go and make sure they're okay, will you? I'm worried." This last part had the force of an order. Molly couldn't help thinking of the old mermaids Serena had gotten to move from the rocks at the clamdunk.

People just did things for Serena without questioning why. And Felicity was probably about to do the same.

Please, Felicity, groaned Molly inwardly. *Honor our pact.*

But her silent pleas were not heeded. Despite Ada's best

efforts to block the door, the combined force of Felicity, Jenna, and Briony was too much.

Felicity's face appeared in the crack first. When she saw that Molly was in her mermaid form, her eyes goggled.

This was the make-or-break moment. The true test of their truce.

Through tear-filled eyes, Molly gazed pleadingly at Felicity, willing her former rival to protect her.

Felicity's decision happened lightning fast. She planted her feet on the ground to stop Jenna and Briony barging in behind her and said, "Everything's fine. We should leave them to it."

"No," said Serena, far too forcefully. "Go in."

Felicity barred the gap in the door with her arms. "No."

"Jenna, Briony?" Serena pushed, although her ethereal tone was marred with quiet desperation.

"Don't," Felicity snapped at them as they tried to shove inside. "If you're really my best friends, you'll go back downstairs, and you'll call my stepdad, and you'll ask him to come and pick me and Molly up."

"But—" said Jenna, obviously baffled by Felicity's staunch defense of the local haddock girl.

Felicity stood her ground. "Now."

Bacon Sandwiches

O nce the bath drain had gurgled empty and Molly had transformed back to her human self, Ada and Felicity escorted her back downstairs to the front door, where Eddie was waiting for them. Serena had gone back into the living room, where she was muttering urgently to Finn. They were probably wondering whether it was obvious what they were up to: whether their cover was blown for good or whether they could try and trick Molly once more.

Felicity's stepdad drove them back to Ada's house in silence. Felicity sat in the front seat, fiddling with the radio. When it was time for them to get out, Molly patted her new ally awkwardly on the shoulder and said, "Thanks." It didn't seem enough, really, but she couldn't go into much detail in front of Felicity's stepdad. She thought the additional "Cheers for not exposing me as a mermaid to my peers and country-men" might raise some questions.

Besides, Eddie didn't know. Not yet anyway.

Did Molly want Eddie to know?

Molly expected herself to freak out at the prospect. If someone had asked her a few weeks ago whether she wanted to share her secret with yet another person, she'd have grabbed Ada by the nostrils and hissed, "Don't tell him I'm a mermaid! For the love of God, don't tell him!"

But she found that she did want Eddie to know. She really, really did.

Being able to discuss her secret openly in front of her best friends would make her life so much easier. If anyone would accept the real her, it would be Eddie.

Plus, she liked him. She liked him a lot. And if anything was ever going to happen between them, she wanted to know beyond all doubt that he was for real. That he was all in when it came to Molly Seabrook. What better way to put that to the test than by showing him the giant slippery fish tail she often had in place of legs?

And so, once Ada's mom and stepdad were in bed, Molly had Ada run her another bath. A very deep one. Then she and Ada ushered Eddie of the Ears into the bathroom, where the three of them waited for the tub to fill.

"Er," he said. "What are we...?"

"I have something to show you," Molly replied, taking a deep, steadying breath as her legs started to tingle.

"Are we getting in the bathtub? Because I have to say, this makes me a little uncomf—"

But before he could finish his sentence, Molly's gleaming white tail had sprung into existence. Ada looked at them both expectantly, waiting for Eddie's reaction.

Eddie's eyes almost popped out of his head. "Excuse me?"

"Erm, I'm a mermaid," Molly said awkwardly.

"Right," he said, nodding as though this was a very normal and obvious development. "Sure. No problem."

All in all, Eddie handled the whole situation remarkably well. Almost too well, in fact. Molly was slightly worried that he had known already. After all, he had always been a big reader of superhero comic books, always been the type to believe in the more fantastical conspiracy theories of this world. Confirming the existence of mermaids was probably deeply satisfying for him. She wouldn't have been surprised if he now dedicated his life to discovering what other paranormal beings existed too.

But what Molly really wanted to know was whether this changed how he felt about her. The temptation to use her merpower was overwhelming.

She could find out. She could find out, once and for all, whether he—and Ada, for that matter—truly accepted her as she was, if she could only manage to access that power. Up until now, it had failed her every time but one.

Okay, think.

How exactly had it gone down at the zoo with Felicity? It hadn't appeared out of nowhere. Something had triggered it.

Molly remembered feeling angrier than she had ever felt, coupled with a deep, dark sense of shame in who she was. The emotions were so potent, they almost blinded her, and soon she felt the exact same emotions emanating from Felicity.

Maybe it was like holding up a mirror. Maybe she really had to lean into her current emotions, and then her merpower would tell her whether her friends' feelings matched hers. That could be why it hadn't worked the last few times she'd tried—because she'd been searching for information, not feelings.

It was worth a try.

Sitting on the bathroom floor next to her two best friends in the world, she reached for it. She reached for it harder than she ever had before.

Closing her eyes for no real reason, Molly tugged on the deep affection she had for her friends. She opened the floodgates of emotion behind those feelings: the trust, the acceptance, the laughs, and the love.

Something in Eddie and Ada responded. Hot and cold gushed through Molly's veins. Her emotions doubled, trebled, until she felt breathless beneath their weight.

They loved her too. They trusted her too. They accepted her too.

Molly's eyes filled with tears. Rather than poking deeper into her best friends' emotions, like she had with Felicity, she let go. She had the only answer she needed. She didn't want to know the intricacies of Eddie's feelings for her or which of their childhood memories Ada held dearest. Some things were better left private.

ℓ·ℓ·ℓ

Molly, Ada, and Eddie spent the rest of the evening drinking horrendous gingerbread coffee, watching old Pixar movies, and talking about the absurd and unreasonable rules of clamdunk. It was perfect.

The next morning, though, Molly returned to the lighthouse, where all her stress and worry came flooding back.

The Seabrooks were in danger. The Waverleys were out to expose them, just as Mom and Margot had suspected all along. They needed to act, but Molly couldn't tell them without admitting they had been right and she had been wrong.

She decided to start with Margot. She was slightly less likely to yell than Mom, although not by much. To sweeten her up, Molly whipped up a batch of bacon sandwiches on soft white bread, loaded a tray with ketchup and pulpy orange juice, then headed up to Margot's room. She somehow managed to rap the secret knock with her one spare knuckle.

Despite the fact that it was after eleven, Margot was still in bed, her covers tangled around her plaid pajamas. She always did this once school broke up for vacation—slept and slept and slept as though she'd never had a single wink in her life until now. Mom had long since given up fighting it and decided she didn't care as long as Margot played her part in the chip shop and kept on top of her schoolwork.

"Morning," Molly said cautiously.

Margot sat bolt upright, her hair a bird's nest on top of her head. She hadn't taken her eyeliner off the night before, and it was smudged all around her eyes like a panda. "What's wrong?"

"What do you mean? Why?"

"You never say morning. You usually just grunt in my direction."

Honestly. There was no getting past Margot and no point in trying. Molly sat down on the edge of the bed, arranged the tray in the middle of the duvet, and picked up a sandwich.

"I messed up," she said, taking such an enormous bite that ketchup plopped straight onto the sheets. Margot looked like she'd never cared about anything less in her life and picked up a sandwich of her own.

"Standard Molly," Margot echoed Ada through a mouthful of crust. "What did you do?"

Molly was so tired she couldn't even be bothered to be nervous. "I went to a party at the Waverleys."

"I'm going to murder you," Margot said matter-of-factly. "Pass me that knife."

"I know, I know," Molly grumbled, licking her fingers. "But I get it now. They're bad news."

"What happened?"

Molly stared intently at the tray. "They tried to trick me into transforming in front of everyone."

"That sounds about right."

Molly gaped at Margot. "You knew?"

"Not for definite. But I had my suspicions."

"How?"

"You know I told you a few weeks back that I don't like the deep sea anymore?"

Margot finished one sandwich and went straight in for another. Molly felt like she should probably offer some to her other sisters before Margot devoured them all. "I used to be the most gung ho Seabrook about exploring. But then last month, I went down for a jaunt one night when I couldn't sleep, and these mermen followed me."

"What?" Shivers ran up and down Molly's arms.

"I think they were...bounty hunters? Or something? They said there was a price on my head and I needed to go with them. They had a huge net. I managed to get away with my merpower, but it was terrifying." Margot shuddered at the memory.

No wonder Molly's sister had been so skittish about going down to Balaena or even just swimming to the clamdunk game. It really wasn't safe.

Margot chewed her bacon thoughtfully. "I think we used to be someone down in Meire, Molly. Criminals, public figures, something like that. And I think that's why Mom doesn't want us going back down there at all. It's not just because of the pollution."

Something clicked into place. The Waverleys were bounty hunters. Clever ones. They bided their time until the right moment, then exposed Molly to her friends. But there was one thing they didn't plan on: how great those friends were. How powerful their bond. How those friends would never betray Molly by taking pictures and reporting her to the authorities.

"Why didn't you tell me?" Molly asked. "About being followed? That's so scary, Margs."

Her sister shrugged. "Because you were only just starting to embrace mermaid life. I didn't want to ruin it for you so soon. I'd had a good few years of loving it before reality hit."

Molly mulled all this over. "There's still so much I don't understand."

"Like what?"

Filling Margot in on the random clues she'd collected— the word *Marefluma*, the hunch about Murielle—Molly finished, "I think you're right. Something happened in Meire that made us leave. Maybe it was to do with who we are or maybe not. But I want to get to the bottom of it."

Dipping in for a third sandwich, Margot exhaled heavily. "Right now, all that can wait. The most pressing thing is, what are we going to do about the Waverleys?"

Molly finished her juice and tucked her feet up under her. "I'm not sure what we can do. I just need to be more careful around them."

"No, Molly." Margot's voice was firm and big sisterly. "They're dangerous. They're going to keep at it until they get what they want, and that's for us to be banished. We can't let that happen."

"So, what do we do?"

A mischievous grin spread across Margot's face. Molly knew right then that a prank was afoot. A jolly big one at that.

"Beat them at their own game."

Tar and Feathers

The plan was foolproof. Almost.

Molly would post on social media that she was working. This involved taking a humiliating haddock-suit selfie and firing it into the ether for the whole of Little Marmouth to see, but it was all for a good cause.

Finn and Serena would inevitably stop by the shop, as they did every time Molly was working. They'd be especially eager today, after Molly had fled the party. They would want to express their fake sympathy that she hadn't been feeling well and gauge whether she was worried about Ada spilling her secret. After all, they had no idea Molly was on to them. As far as they knew, Molly was an idiot and just thought it had all been an unfortunate accident.

Margot would be ready for their arrival.

Sure enough, a mere forty minutes after Molly posted the mortifying shot of herself in a fish costume, the Waverleys rounded the corner, fake grins plastered on their perfect Viking faces. Molly tried to match the jovial look as best she could, despite wanting to smother them in tar and feathers and push them out to sea tied to an inflatable dinghy.

"Molly!" Serena exclaimed, clapping her hands together like a concerned auntie. "You disappeared so fast yesterday. Was everything okay?"

"Yeah," Molly said as casually as she could. A seagull squawked angrily nearby. "I think I ate something funny. Upset stomach."

"You poor thing," Serena simpered. Anger surged in Molly so hot, it took her breath away for a moment. "Did Ada come upstairs and...help you?"

"She did," Molly replied. "Thank you."

"Mind if we get some dinner?" Finn said, nodding toward the chip shop. He didn't notice the CLOSED sign on the door.

Molly smiled for real this time. "Go for it."

The plan was on track.

Waddling in her suit, Molly followed them from the pier toward the chip shop. The second they entered, jangling the welcome bell, Molly pulled the door shut behind them and locked it from the outside. They swiveled to look at her in shock, and she gave them an enthusiastic little thumbs-up through the glass.

They didn't have much time to wonder what was happening. Within seconds, expressions of dawning horror appeared on their faces, and they transformed into mermaids right in the middle of the chip shop. All thanks to the giant vat of defrosted industrial freezer water sitting behind the counter.

What a horrible accident!

Margot was filming them on her phone, her own tail hidden by the counter.

Watching Serena's bloodred tail and Finn's inky black one splash helplessly on the tiled floor gave Molly a sick sense of satisfaction. Revenge was sweet.

Once Margot had secured the footage they needed, she poured away the freezer water. After everyone had transformed back, Molly slipped back into the shop, wiggling the keys triumphantly.

"You little—!" Serena screamed, lunging straight at Molly. Finn caught her by the waist just before she took an eye out.

The vicious reaction made Molly even more smug as she delivered her killing blow. "The way I see it, you have two options," she said. "You either leave Little Marmouth willingly, or my dear friend Ada will contact the authorities.

She's a very fragile human, you see, and was terrified to discover that some of her own schoolmates were supernatural beings. You'll be banished faster than you can say 'karma.'"

Margot grinned triumphantly, replaying the footage on her phone over and over again. It was heavy on the screaming and splashing. "Long story short: you either leave, or you leave. Toodles!"

"Fine," Serena seethed, fury etched all over her face. "We'll go. But sooner or later, your past is going to catch up with you. We aren't the first to come after you, and we certainly won't be the last."

"Cool," Margot said. "Buh-bye now."

"You're cowards," Finn retorted darkly. "All of you. Fleeing your empire the second things get tough. It's shameful. It's treason. And you deserve to rot for it."

"That's a little much," Margot said lightly. "This isn't a Marvel movie, dude."

Finn slammed his fist on the counter, to the point where several Edward sausages tumbled to the front of the cabinet. "You have the audacity to mock? After what your kind did to us?"

Okay, now Molly was lost. "'Your kind'?" she repeated. "We're all mermaids, aren't we?"

Serena spat, actually *spat*, on the floor. "Please. Don't insult us. We're sirens."

Wait. What?

"A war is coming," Finn growled. His chiseled features, white eyes, and sharp teeth made him look like evil person-ified. "A war that's been brewing for thousands of years. You'd better watch your backs." One last sinister smirk. "*Marefluma*."

Adrenaline was coursing through Molly's veins too powerfully for her to figure out what all this meant. But suddenly the Waverleys' magnetic lure and sinister ability to get people to do things for them made a whole lot more sense.

They were sirens. Not mermaids. And Mom had known from the second Margot had described them.

Marefluma

After the showdown in the chip shop, Margot and Molly practically sprinted back to Kittiwake Keep to share what they'd just learned with their sisters. At one point, Margot got a little too close to the edge of the pier, partly transformed into a mermaid, and almost did an Edward off the side of the boardwalk. Thankfully, Molly yanked her back just in time.

Stopping by Melissa's bedroom to grab her en route, the trio then sprinted right up to the top of the lighthouse where Myla's bedroom-cum-library was tucked away from the chaos of the keep. Shockingly, Myla was studying. Boudicca sat on her lap, purring. If Margot was at all surprised to see a house rabbit residing in her sister's room, she hid it well. Melissa, on the other hand...

"Myla! What on earth is that?"

Myla peered up through her glasses. "It's a rabbit, Melissa."

"Well, I can see that!" Melissa crowed in full student supervisor mode. "Does Mom know about this? You know the rules, Myla, no pets unless you're willing to take care of them yourself!"

"I do take care of her myself," Myla answered. "I use my tutoring money to buy her food, and I walk her along the beach three times a day to make sure she's well exercised."

Melissa blinked. "You take her on walks?"

"No, Melissa. She's a rabbit."

Margot snickered at Myla's deadpan tone and flopped onto the extremely messy bed. Molly sat next to her, on top of several textbooks, an empty glasses case, and an old slice of carrot cake with the frosting nibbled off.

Melissa folded her arms. "I still think you should've told Mom."

"Many thanks for your suggestion," Myla said with a sage nod.

"The Waverleys are sirens," Molly interrupted impatiently before telling Myla everything about the confrontation they'd just had. Her sister listened wide-eyed, frowning in places and chewing her lip in others. Meanwhile, Melissa grew redder and redder as she learned of her sisters' antics.

When Molly had finished, Myla said ponderously, "A lot of this makes perfect sense. And a lot of it makes no sense at all." She petted Boudicca like a movie villain stroking a cat.

Melissa took a different tack, face dark as a beet. "Yes, well, I really think you should have listened to Mom and—"

"It wouldn't have been nearly as good a story if we had, would it?" Margot retorted.

"What parts don't make sense, Myla?" Molly asked. Her brain was still in overdrive. How did the Waverleys' secret identities fit into it all?

Myla leaned back in her chair, kicking her feet up on to the desk. "The thing I can't get my head around is that sirens have wings, and the Waverleys most decidedly do not. Sure, now you mention it, the eyes and teeth and bone structure all fit. And the way they had the whole of SPLuM wrapped around their little fingers. But...where are their wings?"

The answer hit Molly like a freight train. "Their scars," she whispered, remembering the perfectly symmetrical white ridges they both had on their shoulder blades. "They had matching scars where wings would be." The thought sent a shudder down her spine. "Did they have them removed? So that they could fit into the human world? If the sea is so bad to live in..."

"Yes," Myla agreed, her tone heavy and fraught. "That

187

would fit. How much do you guys know about the Meire-Syreni conflict?"

Molly gazed at Margot, who looked just as clueless. "Not much. Sorry."

"On this occasion, your ignorance is not your fault."

"Charming," Melissa said.

"I'm serious!" said Myla. "Mom never taught us this stuff, and the only material I've been able to find is written in Mermidian. Would you like the long version or the short version?"

"Short," Margot, Molly, and Melissa all said at once.

"Very well." Myla removed her glasses and began cleaning them meticulously with Boudicca's earlobe. "The mermaids and the sirens have hated each other for thousands of years. Many reasons, really. Some are simple. Most mermaids believe sirens are evil to their core and lure sailors to their deaths, while the sirens maintain that's nothing but propaganda, perpetuated by merministers to fuel anti-siren rhetoric. Which brings me to the more complicated reasons, such as land grabbing and trade sanctions, historic prejudices as well as religious diff—" Myla spotted the zoned-out look on Margot's face. "Sorry, simple version. Mermaids no likey sirens. Sirens no likey mermaids. Capisce?"

"Capisce," Margot confirmed begrudgingly.

"According to further reading I've been doing, this was all compounded when, twenty years ago, the queen of Meire negotiated our asylum with the humans," Myla continued. "Records show that she had the opportunity to include the sirens in the deal, but she chose not to. She left them in the sea, with no way out."

Finn's words ricocheted around Molly's mind. *"You have the audacity to mock? After what your kind did to us?"*

He'd also said a war was coming. And now, with a deep, sinking feeling, Molly understood why. She didn't blame them. All right, so the mermaids and the sirens didn't like each other. Still, it was pretty messed up that the mermaid queen had the chance to help their fellow sea dwellers and chose not to.

This went part of the way toward explaining why Mom was so fearful of them going in the sea. If they were at risk of being attacked by vengeful sirens, no wonder she was overly protective.

It was all starting to make sense...with one exception.

"What about Marefluma?" Molly asked, almost dreading the answer. "Finn and Serena hissed it at us before they left, as though it was a curse word."

Myla replaced her glasses, a conflicted look on her face. "This is where it gets hard to hear the truth. Are you sure you're ready?"

Margot snorted. "Do you honestly expect us to say no and go back downstairs?"

"I suppose not. Very well. Have you ever studied Latin?" Myla asked in her best wacky-professor voice.

"Have you ever met me before?" Molly snorted. "I struggle even to study English. Or the Chinese takeout menu."

Myla rubbed her hands as though approaching a very juicy plate of pork kung po. Or, well, a very juicy stack of textbooks. This was Myla they were talking about. "Well, in Latin, the word *mare* can be translated as 'sea.'"

"Okay..." Molly said uncertainly.

"And *flumen*...any ideas?"

Molly racked her brain. Flume seemed too obvious. Flute? She supposed they were vaguely like telescopes. "Nope. Tell me."

"*Flumen* means 'river,'" Myla finished.

Molly felt very stupid for not immediately understanding. "Right."

Myla waited for a moment, then realized her slow sister was not going to get there on her own. Neither were Margot and Melissa, who were also staring blankly at her. She sighed and said, "Can you think of any other English synonyms for 'river'?"

"Uh, stream...wait." Goose bumps trailed up and down Molly's arms. "Wait. It's brook."

"Marefluma," Myla murmured. "Seabrook."

Oh my goodness. *Oh my goodness.*

In the book she'd read, Marefluma had been used as a surname for the past five empresses. Mira Marefluma. Marilla Marefluma. Myra Marefluma. Morwenna Marefluma. Mericia Marefluma.

"We were royalty?" Molly gasped, struggling to stay quiet now. Surely Mom, who was pottering around making soup downstairs, could hear?

"We were royalty," Myla confirmed.

Margot swore colorfully.

Thousands of dazzling questions tore through Molly's head, so fast she couldn't pluck one out from the noise. Her mind fizzed. "So, what happened? Does that mean Murielle is still...queen? Empress?"

"I don't know," Myla admitted. "She was when we left, I believe. But after we fled, she had no heirs, and she was getting older by the day. It's possible she's been overthrown, but without contact with her or Meire in general, we have no way of knowing. There's no Google for this stuff, and all our books are outdated."

"She was when we left," Melissa repeated slowly. A look of dawning horror had appeared on her face, and Molly didn't like it one little bit.

"What? What's wrong?" Margot asked.

Myla's gaze was laden with something like shame. The final truth hit Molly.

"Murielle negotiated the deal with the humans," Molly said sadly. "She condemned the sirens to the sea when she could've helped. That's why there was a big fight between her and Mom. That's why the Waverleys hate us so much." A gulp. "That's why all the sirens do."

Rumors of Sugar Cookies

The whole Seabrook clan spent that cold, snowy Sunday evening decorating Kittiwake Keep for Christmas. This largely involved Minnie getting herself tangled in Christmas lights and farting from hysteria.

Unfortunate bodily functions aside, it was always one of Molly's favorite nights of the year: the scent of drying oranges in the oven, the sound of the same five songs playing on the radio, the warmth of the fire, and the crunch of tinsel as Margot wrapped herself in it from head to toe and pretended to be a glitter yeti, which only made Minnie happy-fart even more. Myla harping on about the history of yuletide ("Did you know Prince Albert introduced the Germanic tradition of indoor Christmas trees at Windsor Castle in 1841?") and Melissa insisting that this was the year they should finally add cranberry-stuffed cod to the fish menu.

The doorbell chimed, and Melissa went to answer it. She came back into the living room with Ada, Eddie, and...Amy Fairbairn.

Myla stood up, cheeks flushing. "Amy. You came."

Amy grinned, tucking a lock of ginger hair behind her ear. "Of course. I heard rumors of sugar cookies."

Myla crossed the room, stepping over a mess of baubles and ornaments, so she was standing next to Amy. She smiled self-consciously. "Guys, this is Amy. My girlfriend."

The room erupted into awws and squeals, even from Ada and Eddie of the Ears.

"I'm so happy for you, Myla!" Melissa gushed, throwing her arms around her older sister.

"That's amazing!" Margot said, although of course she'd already known.

"Congrats, you guys," said Eddie of the Ears. He was looking at Molly in a wistful sort of way.

"What's a girlfriend?" Minnie asked. She was wearing jelly shoes, even in the depths of winter. "And where do babies come from?"

"Amy, I hope you know what you're getting yourself into with the Seabrooks," Molly said. "We are not normal people."

"That's a relief." Amy beamed knowingly. "I'm not normal people, either." She looked over to where Margot was standing dressed as a glitter yeti. "Did you know that modern tinsel was invented in Nuremberg in 1610 and was originally made of shredded silver?"

Margot grinned. "You and Myla are perfect for each other."

Amy and Myla laced their hands together, then said simultaneously, "We know."

They all proceeded to deck out the Keep with the most inappropriate quantity of decorations anyone had ever seen. Margot glued upside-down silver candlesticks to the ceiling, Amy and Myla made a neat wreath out of ribbons, holly, and pine cones, while Eddie helped Melissa hang the hideous homemade clay ornaments on the wonky tree.

As she watched her family unapologetically being her family, Molly's eyes filled with tears. She had nearly ruined all this. She had nearly thrown it all away. And for what?

She had to tell her mom the truth. It was the only way to get rid of this awful, roiling guilt and start over with a clean slate.

She padded through to the kitchen where Mom was poring over a turkey pie recipe. Her slippered foot was tapping along to "All I Want for Christmas Is You," and she had her festive reindeer apron tied around her waist.

"Mom, I'm sorry," Molly choked out.

Mom frowned, then melted when she saw the sad state of her daughter. She wrapped Molly up in a big, orange-scented hug. "Oh, sweetie, whatever for?"

They sat down at the table, covered in frosting and cookie dough and half-empty mugs of milky tea, and Molly told her mom everything. Well, apart from the clamdunk plan. That was Margot's sword to fall on.

Rushing through it all, Molly described the last few weeks, from serving the Waverleys in the shop to sneaking out to the house party. She grew breathless as she flew through the story. Mom's eyes bulged when Molly explained about the bubble-bath trap and the way she and Margot had gotten even and forced the Waverleys out of town. Then, when Molly talked about how she and her sisters had put the puzzle together and figured out the truth about Marefluma, Mom looked positively astounded—and also a little impressed.

"I'm sorry," Molly sobbed when she was finally done. She propped her elbows on the table and dropped her head into her hands. "You were right. I should've listened."

Mom seemed to be weighing her words, searching for the exact right ones. Eventually, she said, "Well, thank you for being honest. You're right, you should've told me. That stunt you and Margot pulled was very dangerous, not to mention morally questionable."

"I know." Molly sniffed. "We just didn't know what else to do. And I made the mess, so I wanted to clean it up myself. I'm sorry. Please don't hate me."

"Hate you?" Now Mom's voice was the one to wobble. She gently eased Molly's hands out from under her chin, then gave them a squeeze. "Molly, I could never hate you. In fact, I love how strong-willed you all are. I really do. You all have such fierce personalities, and it's wonderful. But you have to trust me. I know what's best for this family. I'm never just strict for the sake of being strict. There's always a reason. And sometimes I can't share that reason with you. Please believe me when I say that I have your best interests at heart."

Molly wiped away a tear and smirked. "That's very...regal of you."

"Nice try," Mom said but with a smile.

"Mom, please," Molly begged. "You have to meet me halfway."

Mom shook her head kindly. "No, I don't. You're thirteen, Molly. Our past is a dark and rocky one, and it won't do you any good hearing the gory details. All you need to know is that things between the mermaids and the sirens are very complicated, and your grandmother Murielle made it even more so. She and I no longer speak for that very reason."

"Is she still queen?" Molly asked.

"She is still queen," Mom confirmed.

Which makes us royalty, too, Molly thought to herself.

Mom smiled gently. "We'll talk it all through sometime, Molly. I promise. Should we just enjoy ourselves for now?"

With the sound of sisterly chaos ringing in the background, Molly smiled. "Okay"

They all spent the next half hour being taught an extremely convoluted mermaid board game by Myla, who had read about it in one of her books and re-created a set. Unfortunately, it involved seventeen dice, three decks of snapfish cards, and a troubling number of trivia quizzes, so eventually they gave up and decided to make fudgy hot cocoa to sip by the fire.

It was all very sweet and merry and made Molly think that maybe normal life wasn't so bad, after all.

Being royalty could wait. Besides, she'd just found a piece of fudge from last week in her ponytail, so there was a chance she wasn't quite ready for a princess-y existence just yet. Regal was not her style.

However, just as they'd wrapped up in blankets to watch a Christmas movie, there was another ring of the doorbell.

"I wonder who this could be now?" Mom said, rising to

her feet. "Does Melissa have a secret boyfriend or girlfriend we didn't know about? Or do we think Margot has egged the arcade again? Honestly, one of these days, I'm just going to let the police take her."

They went through into the hallway to find out who this surprise visitor was. A cold draft told them the door was already open. Margot, Myla, and Melissa stood frozen to the doormat, with Minnie wriggling excitedly between their legs.

Molly saw a haggard old woman with long, straggly hair standing on the doorstep. She wore an extravagant necklace with a golden seahorse pendant and had one arm wrapped in a sling made of seaweed. All around her were stacks of battered old suitcases and handbags, as though she were planning to stay at Kittiwake Keep for a long while.

She stared straight at Mom with unblinking, sea-blue eyes.

"Murielle," croaked Mom. "What are you doing here?"

"I'm coming to live with you," barked their strange grandmother. She looked around the chaos of the lighthouse—the abandoned dice, the spilled hot cocoa, a curious hamster sniffing at a lump of week-old hair fudge. Murielle's nose wrinkled in disgust. "You girls are royalty. *Princesses.* And you'd better start acting like it."

Minnie frowned. "We're not princesses. We're just the Seabrooks. And why do you smell like fish?"

About the Author

Laura Kirkpatrick is part mermaid, part children's author, and she lives in northern England. Her favorite things are white chocolate, beach walks with her puppy, and hiding her tail from prying humans. In addition to her fiction, Laura is a journalist and screenwriter.